---------------- ★ ----------------

Sharyn got out of the Jeep and walked back to cabin number five. The side door was open, but there was no sign of anyone else having been there. She walked inside cautiously and looked around the room. Everything looked the same.

She went back outside and studied the front door that opened into the wall. There was something odd about it. When she pushed against the wall where the door opened, she heard something groan inside the cabin. She went back inside and pushed at the wall again, definitely feeling something give way.

A shadow passed by on the ceiling and Sharyn felt a prickle of fear at the base of her neck. There was a loud groan from the roof timbers but before she could move, the entire ceiling came crashing down on her. She put up her arms to ward off the worst of the weight from hitting her head, but there was too much material. The supporting timber knocked her to the floor and she was buried beneath the rubble of wood and shingles. Sunlight danced on the dust motes as the wood settled, and then was still.

---------------- ★ ----------------

For the Last Time

JOYCE & JIM LAVENE

W🌐RLDWIDE®

TORONTO • NEW YORK • LONDON
AMSTERDAM • PARIS • SYDNEY • HAMBURG
STOCKHOLM • ATHENS • TOKYO • MILAN
MADRID • WARSAW • BUDAPEST • AUCKLAND

Recycling programs
for this product may
not exist in your area.

FOR THE LAST TIME

A Worldwide Mystery/February 2013

First published by Avalon Books

ISBN-13: 978-0-373-26834-4

Copyright © 2002 by Joyce & Jim Lavene

Printed in U.S.A.

For our daughter and personal editor, Jennifer, who has faithfully read all of the Sharyn Howard manuscripts and added so much to them.
Thanks for all of your great ideas.
We love you!

Bell's Creek, though created by God, has surely been cursed by Him. This past winter has been the coldest in memory. Many died through lack of common necessities. Spring has finally arrived but it has brought with it more tragedy. This very day, God's day, when we would have baptized thirty of the Faithful, the creek rose suddenly from the spring thaw in the mountains. All thirty were lost, along with the pastor, Robert J. Hanford. Not a single body was recovered from the icy torrent. I shall succeed him in the pulpit, preaching to the Faithful. But I know this land is cursed. May God have mercy on all our souls and smile upon us once more.

John Abbott, Pastor
Bell's Creek Presbyterian Church—1870

ONE

"FOR THE LAST MONTH, the old Bell's Creek campground here in Montgomery County has been a hive of activity. College students from across the state, as well as local officials, have taken part in the renovation of this once-popular site. Behind us is the shadow of Diamond Mountain, the highest peak in the Uwharries. And here with us now is state senator Caison Talbot, who— Ouch!"

The pretty, blond television reporter stumbled when her foot twisted in a hole in the soggy ground. She reached out to catch herself but nothing was there. The cameraman tried to help her but it was too late. She was on the ground, covered in mud. She picked up her lost shoe and looked at the broken heel.

"That's just great! How am I supposed to do this interview covered in mud and who knows what else? I'm going to have to shower and change and—"

"Nonsense!" Senator Talbot assured her. "You'll be fine! Just brush yourself off."

"I'm covered in mud, Senator!" she replied through clenched teeth. "I'll only be a few minutes once we get to the motel."

Talbot's eyes widened. He shook his head. "No one's going to be looking at *you!* We'll be done here by the time you get back! I'll have to give the interview to someone else." He looked around at the swarm of television and newspaper reporters as though he were trying to decide which lucky one was going to interview him.

"Oh, all right," the woman said. "Give me a minute. Shawn, keep that camera angle away from this side!"

"You got it," the photographer said, putting down the heavy camera until his leading lady was ready.

"I'll wash my face and then we can talk. It shouldn't be more than a few minutes, Senator."

Talbot glanced at his watch. "Time's wasting, young woman!"

The reporter ground her teeth, remembered her expensive dental work, and then marched towards the cabin that had been designated for use by the workers and the press.

Sharyn Howard and her sister, Kristie, watched the attractive woman walk past them, muttering beneath her breath. The reporter was wearing only one shoe, and she was covered in dark orange mud.

"Wonder what's wrong with her," Kristie wondered aloud as she swept her paintbrush up and down the side of the old wooden cabin.

"What makes you think something was wrong?" Sharyn asked, trying her best to paint as efficiently as her sister.

Kristie stared at her. "You're my sister, the sheriff, right? You're the one who notices things and solves crimes, right?"

"Only when I'm working," Sharyn replied calmly. She wiped a trickle of sweat from her forehead and left a trail of mint green paint on her face. "The rest of the time, I'm blissfully ignorant."

Kristie laughed. "You're a mess! Who gave you that paintbrush?"

Sharyn rubbed at the paint on her face and made it worse. "I think it was Keith."

"I'll have to talk to him." Kristie smiled at her sister. "I wanted to thank you for all your help again. I couldn't have gotten this campground project up and running without you."

"I don't know how much help I really was, seeing as it's turned into a media circus for the elections."

"They came. They painted and took out trash. That's what counted."

Sharyn glanced at her. "I'm proud of you for setting this whole thing up for the kids, Kristie. It was a good thing to do."

They painted in silence for a few more minutes

while the blond reporter stalked past them again, this time missing both shoes. Neither sister paid much attention to her. The sun was hot for April. The temperatures were unseasonably warm after a short, cold winter. The sky was clear and blue. The weather had worked with them while they restored the old campground. Not a single day of rain in two weeks.

All but three of the old cabins were painted. They'd come as close as they could to the original colors of yellow, orange, and green. The campground was over a hundred years old but most of the buildings were in pretty good shape. The three that weren't would be kept off limits until they could be demolished. They were a strange hodgepodge of heights and sizes, all stacked together with odd balconies that ran into blank walls and doorways that opened into empty halls that went nowhere.

"Keith told me that the cabins were built like this to confuse the devil," Kristie told her sister, their minds traveling along similar pathways.

"That was probably a good idea since the old stories confirm that this is the most wicked part of the county," Sharyn agreed.

Kristie dipped her paintbrush into the paint bucket. "You like him, don't you?"

"The devil?" Sharyn wondered, teasing her.

"No! Keith!" Kristie made a face. "Like you didn't know who I was talking about!"

"He's nice," Sharyn told her sister. "He seems… nice."

"Is that it?" Kristie wondered. "Is that the only thing you can find to say about him?"

Sharyn was about to answer when a loud scream pierced the drowsy campground.

"I'll bet that was the reporter again!" Kristie said, putting down her paintbrush. "I'll bet something happened to her!"

Her sister continued to paint as though nothing had happened.

"Well?"

"Well…what?"

Kristie squinted at Sharyn. "Don't you want to run over there and see what happened? I mean you *are* the sheriff and everything! Suppose—"

"Sheriff! Come quick! That lady reporter who's been trying to interview Senator Talbot just tripped over something else!"

"Something else like what?" Sharyn asked her newest deputy, J. P. Santiago.

"We're not sure. But Ernie said to come and get you!"

Sharyn looked at her deputy in his blue jeans and red T-shirt covered in paint. Then she smiled at her sister. "You see? I don't have to run. They come for me."

Kristie smirked. "Some election poster that would make! The sheriff of Montgomery County: she takes her time getting to the scene of your crime!"

"Hey, when you're sheriff, you can criticize," Sharyn told her, wiping her hands on a cloth. She started walking with J. P. towards the front of the old camp. "Until then—"

They rounded the corner of one group of cabins. All of the press that was covering the elections from the county and the state were waiting there, watching for her. Cameras flashed as she walked towards the throng.

Sharyn self-consciously smoothed down her old T-shirt and baggy overalls, wishing she were wearing her uniform. A badge and a gun made all the difference. Most of the time, she hated the ugly tan-and-brown uniform that looked terrible on her. Today, it might be nice to hide behind it.

She could imagine the whispered speculation in the crowd as she walked to the edge of the compound. *So that's Sharyn Howard! She doesn't have anyone running against her in the primary so she didn't even have to declare yet. She hasn't done anything that says, "I'm running for sheriff*

*again." Maybe that's why she's here today with
the other candidates.*

Added to that speculation were other random
thoughts. *Gee, her hair sure is red! She sure has
a lot of freckles! She could stand to lose a few
pounds! How tall is she?*

"Sheriff," Ernie said when he saw her. He and
Annie, his fiancé, were supporting the reporter between them. "I think her ankle might be broken."

Sharyn nodded, putting all the other thoughts
behind her. "J.P.? Call for an ambulance, please."

"Yes, ma'am," the deputy said, taking out his
new cell phone. He'd only been with the sheriff's
office a few months. His wife teased him about
sleeping with his badge and his cell phone but it
was the most important job he'd ever had and he
was proud to be there.

"What did you trip over?" Sharyn asked, glancing into the clearing behind them.

"I'm not sure, but it hurt," the reporter told her.
"I was walking with the senator. He was telling
me about the reclamation of the property. We were
looking at that area over there where they've cleared
the kudzu and undergrowth. Then 'boom.' I fell
across it."

Sharyn nodded. "Why don't you help her sit
down at the table over there, Ernie? Then we'll see
what went 'boom.'"

Senator Talbot was standing beside Sharyn's mother. His shock of white hair and ruddy face made his blue eyes stand out. Both the senator and her mother were dressed as though they'd just come from a church social, but that didn't surprise Sharyn. After all, neither one of them had done anything that day but pass out lemonade and smile for the cameras.

"Sharyn, what *is* that on your face?" Faye Howard whispered as her daughter walked by her.

"Paint, Mom," Sharyn confided. "I was painting."

"Here?" her mother hissed. "Everyone knows I'm marrying the senator when the election is over! What will they think?"

"Not to mention your own campaign," Caison Talbot reminded Sharyn briskly. "If I didn't know better, I'd think you were trying to lose the election."

"I haven't even declared yet," Sharyn answered in turn. "Excuse me. I need to see what almost ate the reporter."

Ernie, her head deputy, joined her as the group stood around in the late afternoon sun and watched them walk across the cleared but uneven ground.

"What are we looking for?" J.P. asked, joining them.

"Something big enough to trip a reporter, presumably to make good press coverage," Ernie replied. "Could be a tree stump. Could be an old moonshine still. Could be—"

"A suitcase," Sharyn said.

Ernie shrugged. "Could be, I guess, but it seems unlikely, doesn't it?"

"No." Sharyn pointed to the brown square sticking up out of the ground. "It *is* a suitcase."

Out of habit, she put on the gray work gloves she'd worn earlier when she was helping pull weeds from around the cabins. She tugged at the suitcase and it came free from the soft ground.

"The bulldozer must've pushed it up out of the ground," Ernie speculated. "Looks like it's been out here awhile."

Sharyn laid the suitcase down on the ground. It was small, maybe two feet across and two feet high. It was made of some heavy, coarse material that had moldered in a few places.

"Is it a body?" someone called out from the crowd.

"Hardly," Sharyn answered. "It's an old suitcase."

"Is somebody inside of it?" Foster Odom yelled from behind her. The crowd laughed a little, and then started to disperse.

Sharyn didn't bother to answer again. The handle and clasps were intact on the suitcase. There was even a small brass lock that was corroded. She tried to open it but it wouldn't budge. She wiped her hand over the top of it. The red clay had leached into the material but there were stains that were darker on the top and sides.

"Probably some child left it here when the camp was open last," J.P. said quietly. "Why was the camp closed for so long?'

Ernie glanced at Sharyn. "There was a murder. It goes along with this being the most evil part of the county."

"Evil?" J.P. asked with a smile. "That's a word people don't use much anymore."

Ernie brushed his hands together to clean them off. "Out here, they do."

J.P. looked at Sharyn. "Sheriff? Is this an evil place?"

Sharyn picked up the suitcase. "It's a bunch of old stories, J.P. I know you've seen those tourist flyers about the haunted Uwharries? Well, a lot of those stories came from here. Devil's Campground, people used to call this old place."

"Used to?" Ernie snorted. "A lot of them still do!"

"Devil's Campground," J.P. considered. "That sounds evil."

"I think the stories are the only things that are really evil around here," Sharyn told them. "I'm going to take this back to town and let Nick and his students play around with it."

"Sounds good," Ernie agreed.

"I'm going back to painting," J.P. said. "I'm glad it wasn't something worse." He looked at the reporters milling around the camp. "I don't think *they* are, though."

Ernie smiled. He glanced at Annie, who was still with the reporter. The sunlight was in her golden hair and his heart swelled with his love for her. He looked back at Sharyn, who was still examining the old suitcase. "You miss him?"

Sharyn didn't look up. "Who?"

"Who? Like you don't know who I'm talking about!"

"I'm going to put this in my Jeep," she told him. "When Nick gets back from vacation tomorrow, he can have it to trick his students."

"You know, you never were much of a liar," Ernie told her as she walked away.

"Do I tell you what you should do with your personal life?" she asked him without looking back.

"When I let you!"

She shook her head and continued walking.

The ambulance arrived for the reporter who was willing to agree with Bell's Creek's reputation for evil. Senator Talbot found another reporter only too happy to give him an exclusive interview. Sharyn stowed the suitcase and returned to her painting. Kristie was gone. Her bucket and brush were still there but she had disappeared. It wasn't difficult to imagine where she'd gone since Keith Reynolds was there at the campground. He and Kristie had been together almost constantly during spring break.

Sharyn considered what Ernie had said about Nick. Part of it was teasing, she knew, but part of it was serious, too. He was concerned that she was going to be alone when her mother married Senator Talbot at the end of the year. Kristie was away at college or traveling around the country with various projects. Her father, Sheriff T. Raymond Howard, had been gone for almost three years after being gunned down at a local convenience store.

Nick Thomopolis was the medical examiner for Montgomery County. He'd worked with her father before her. He and Sharyn had worked together for the past three years. It had been a stormy relationship at first, but lately, it seemed to be evolving into something more.

Sharyn brushed the green paint evenly across the weather-beaten wood. In her own mind and heart, she'd stopped kidding herself. She did care for Nick but she wasn't sure he felt the same about her. And she wasn't sure it was a good idea for the sheriff to start dating the medical examiner. Although with her schedule, a date might have to consist of a sandwich while talking over county business.

Of course, all of that could be about to change. It was election year, complete with hundreds of little flags and banners around town. Each one touted a different candidate with a picture and a few words about why they were the best for the job. Those whispers she'd caught from the crowd were valid. None of those flags or banners had her name on them. She hadn't made a formal declaration that she was running for sheriff again. The other party was setting up their own candidate for sheriff. Her party was still waiting for some word from her.

"Sheriff?"

Sharyn jumped a little and smeared paint sideways across the wall. She looked at the man who'd startled her. "Hello, Mr. Odom."

"Call me Foster," the reporter for the *Diamond Springs Gazette* told her. "I'll call you Sharyn."

"That's okay," she responded with little enthusiasm. The man had made a nuisance of himself ever since he'd come to work at the *Diamond Springs Gazette.*

"I'd like to be friends," he insisted. "We *are* in the same business."

"What's that?"

"Keeping up with the public. Making sure they're

safe and informed. I'd like to help you do that for another four years in Diamond Springs."

Sharyn stopped painting and stared at him. "I read the paper, Mr. Foster. You've called for my resignation twice!"

"And I paid my debt to society when I spent the night in your jail."

"You were the one who came into the impound lot when the signs warned you to stay out!"

"And didn't I help out by reporting about that situation for you? I made taxpayers aware that you needed more money to get extra security," he replied.

"Yes you did," she agreed. "By telling them that the impound lot was run by an old dinosaur who couldn't see his hand in front of his face! What we ended up with, as I'm sure you know, is Charlie being retired by the county commission and no new funding for help to take his place."

Foster shrugged. He was wearing the same casual tan polyester suit that had come to be his trademark around town. His Charlotte Panthers ball cap was pulled down low on his chubby face; his long, pale hair was tied back on his neck. "I did what I thought was right. Just like you do, Sheriff."

"Not exactly." She dipped her brush in paint and started back painting again.

"I haven't made you and Dr. Thomopolis an item, like some people."

"I would rather you'd done that than get Charlie fired."

"Did you want him to work there forever?" Foster Odom argued. "He needed to retire. I'll bet he's reveling in it!"

"Follow up on your story, Mr. Odom," Sharyn told him bluntly. "He's in the hospital with pneumonia."

"You can't blame me for that, Sheriff!" He smiled, then stopped and shook his head when she didn't return his smile. "Anyway, this is different. Don't you think everyone's noticed that you haven't declared your candidacy for sheriff? Don't you think everyone's wondering what's going on? I can help you reach the people and say what you want to say, Sheriff. I could be a great ally!"

"No, thanks," she answered. "When I'm ready to announce what I'm doing, I'll call a press conference. Until then, I don't need your help."

"Sheriff—"

"Shouldn't you be interviewing someone?" she asked pointedly.

"Fine! I can offer my services to your competition. Mr. Tarnower is a man who has an eye for a photo op. He wouldn't be standing here, painting in obscurity, while the real advantage is being up there with the crowd. People didn't even know you were here! Did you know that? They were surprised to see you when you came walking out! I'm pretty sure that's the only reason your deputy called you up that way. What kind of press do you think that's going to get you?"

"The kind I want, Mr. Odom," she said. "None at all."

He left her alone. Sharyn painted vigorously for a few more minutes, then she looked at her watch and decided to call it a day. She put a top on her bucket of paint and cleaned her brush. Keith and Kristie emerged from the storage room looking flushed and happy.

"Thanks, Sheriff," Keith said. "Kristie and I both appreciate your help on the campground."

He was a quiet boy with a receding hairline at twenty-five and glasses that gave him an air of spending too much time at the computer. He'd been with Nick most of the time since he'd transferred to the local college. He had hopes of someday becoming a medical examiner.

"You're welcome." She glanced at her starry-eyed sister. "I think your brush and bucket are still out there."

"Oh." Kristie giggled. "Yeah. I'll go get them."

"I'll come, too," Keith offered.

"They're cute together," Caison said, coming into

the building as he passed them. He handed Sharyn the empty lemonade jug. "Your mother is concerned about Kristie's education but I think she'll be fine."

Sharyn put the lemonade pitcher on a shelf. Maybe Ernie was right, she speculated. Maybe Caison was good for her mother.

"It's you I'm worried about," he contended. His bright blue eyes bored through her. "Are you going to run for sheriff again?"

"I don't actually have to decide that yet. August eighteenth is the last filing day," she told him.

She didn't want to discuss this with him. He'd been a friend of her parents' for years before her father was killed. Ernie had assured her that Caison was a better man than she wanted to acknowledge. But no matter what, there was something about him that she didn't like and didn't trust. He smelled of too many late-night, backroom deals and too much power. He'd been the state senator from their district for almost twelve years. She knew he stayed there because he was a power broker. He knew where the secrets were buried and he didn't mind using his influence to make sure they stayed buried. Or were found at the worst times.

"So, you aren't going to run?" he continued, frowning down on her.

Sharyn faced him with quiet dignity. "I'm not sure which side of this fence you're on, Senator!

I know you're friends with the D.A. I know he's supporting Roy Tarnower. He's been pretty vocal about it. I know he doesn't want me to be sheriff for another four years. Are you interested in this because I might decide to run again? Or because you're supposed to help convince me that I shouldn't run again?"

The rage in Senator Talbot's tanned face should have been enough to burn her to a cinder. "Frankly, I don't care what you do, Sharyn! But your mother is counting on the fact that you won't run again and break her heart! I don't know what's going on with Jack Winter! But if you weren't so selfish, you'd go ahead and decide so that your mother's mind would be at ease!"

Sharyn's face felt hot. She knew it wasn't from standing in the sun that day. No amount of sun block could keep her freckled face from showing her anger and embarrassment that the senator would talk to her this way!

"If you *are* working with my mother on this, Senator, tell her that I love her, but I'm like my father. It takes me a while to make a decision. And if you're working with D.A. Winter, tell him that he can't buy me, scare me, or make my decision for me. I'm going to do what I think is best for me and this town!" She left him there, so angry that she didn't even see Ernie until she'd almost run him over.

"What's wrong?" he asked.

"Nothing," she muttered. "I'm going home. I'll see you at the office tomorrow."

"I know you better! Have you been talking to your mama again?"

"Tomorrow, Ernie," she told him again, opening the door to her Jeep. "Say good-bye to Annie for me."

Ernie frowned as he watched her drive away. He'd watched her grow up for the past twenty-nine years. Her daddy, the previous sheriff, T. Raymond Howard, had been proud of her. She could shoot straight and think clearly. Ernie still wondered if old T. Raymond didn't always want her to be sheriff. He'd sent her off to law school but Ernie knew T. Raymond hated lawyers. Maybe he'd always wanted her to take his place.

Not so soon, mind you. Ernie knew T. Raymond didn't think the first thing his young daughter would do, as sheriff, would be to investigate her father's murder. He could still see the look on her face when she'd come into that store and her daddy was lying on the floor. She'd been the first woman elected sheriff in North Carolina history. He knew it was hard for her at first but he also knew she'd gained everyone's respect in her first term of office. He just didn't know what was going through her mind about running again. And that's what scared him!

SHARYN WENT HOME and showered. She tossed her old clothes into the wash and pulled on a soft cream-colored T-shirt and jeans. She looked into the mirror and made sure her face was clean. Then she picked up a book she'd been trying to finish for the past month. Most people didn't know it but she was a closet romance reader. She didn't drag the paperbacks with the passionate covers around with her. They mostly waited for a quiet time in her life.

Those times were becoming increasingly difficult to find. As the county grew with refugees from Charlotte, their nearest big city, so did the crime rate. The county was waiting for the tax increase they expected from the young, upper-income families to catch up with law enforcement and schools. In the meantime, the sheriff's department workload doubled with only a few extra people to help bear the brunt of the work.

Diamond Springs, with its sparkling clear lake, ringed by the ancient Uwharrie Mountains, was also becoming more popular with tourists. They brought in their own problems during the season from June to October. There had been an influx of non-English-speaking workers that had created a whole new set of challenges. In short, the area wasn't the same place that her father had watched over for twenty years. Her grandfather, Jacob, had been sheriff for thirty years before him.

The job had passed down to her. It hadn't been a matter of conscious choice. Shocked by her father's untimely death, Sharyn had listened to the voices that urged her to run for his position. People in the county knew and trusted the name. And even though she was a woman, the people had voted for her in the special election. She didn't know how many had voted for her out of pity because of her father's death. She would probably never know. She'd done her best to serve, but with the new election came new questions.

Her mother had asked her not to run again. She'd told Sharyn that she was afraid every time she went to work. She'd reminded Sharyn that she'd gone to law school and if her father had lived, she would have been a lawyer. There was the future to think about and the past to understand. Did she really want to be sheriff? She'd brought her father's killers to justice. She'd solved a few murders and settled a few disputes during her four years as sheriff. Was she ready to move on? Life had changed. Did she want to go back and take the bar exam to become a lawyer? Or was she satisfied being sheriff of Diamond Springs?

Ernie, Kristie, Nick, and a few others had told her that she should run, no matter what. Sharyn wasn't so sure. She was still in turmoil about the whole thing.

Sighing, she sat back against her headboard and pulled out her romance novel. The heroine had been trapped by her lover's deadly rival for far too long. She wasn't going to think about it anymore that night. She was going to sit back and read her book.

But an hour later, Sharyn was on her way back out of the house. Kristie and her mother were still out with Caison and Keith. The heroine in the novel was still trapped. She sighed and looked up at the stars. She might have to settle her own life before she could be much use to the other woman in the book. She was on her way to the office, thinking that she could get started on some paperwork for the next day. Then she thought about the suitcase in the back of her Jeep and took the turn that led to the hospital. She would leave it with a note on Nick's desk at the morgue. That way, she wouldn't have to think about remembering to take it to him. Otherwise, a month later, she could still be riding around with it in her Jeep.

Nick's office was locked. He'd been on vacation for the past two weeks. It had happened at a good time since he was the only M.E. they had in the county. Things had been quiet. They only got a few murders a year. The rest of the time, he taught forensics and psychology at the local college. For the last six months, he'd used his students to help him when the M.E.'s office got busy. He'd tried hiring

an assistant but the outcome was worse than working alone. The county still had the money available
for him to hire an assistant. Sharyn thought Keith
Reynolds might be his next choice.

She used her key to open his door, then switched
on the light. Carefully, she put the heavy, dirty suitcase on a chair, then looked for paper to write a
note. She began to look at all the personal things
in his office.

He'd been in the Navy. Sharyn knew that much.
She looked at his commendations on the wall. He'd
left the Navy as a lieutenant. There was a picture of
him in uniform with some other men and women
around him. It was black and white and it didn't
do him justice. His hair looked dark and his eyes
were obscured.

He had licenses on the wall to practice psychology and forensics. He had pictures of what looked to
be his family. He never talked about his family that
he'd left behind in New York. She'd never known
him to go and visit them. His vacations were usually
conferences and seminars. The county commission
had made him take this vacation after two years
without one. He hadn't been pleased with that order.

He had a model plane on his desk. She laughed
at that because he was afraid to fly. Of course, he'd
been in the Navy and he was afraid of water. The
man was a mass of contradictions.

She sat down in his big chair and put her feet up on his desk, as she'd seen him do so many times. Nick always seemed to be at ease. He was always calm, sarcastic, and, in her case, ready to take offense. He was a good M.E. and a good friend. Was she really interested in him being any more than that to her?

There was a noise at the door. Before she could sit up, it opened.

"Well!" Nick put down his bag. "I'm gone for two weeks and you're already taking over my space!"

TWO

SHARYN ALMOST FELL out of the chair trying to get up quickly. "Nick! I wasn't expecting you back so soon! How was your vacation?"

"It was all right, considering it was either go, or stay in my apartment for two weeks and watch old videos. What are you doing here? Have you decided to try your hand at forensics instead of running for sheriff?"

"I'm, uh—" She untangled her foot from the phone cord. "I was dropping off this suitcase that we found out at the old campground today." She found her footing again in expressing the basics. "I thought you and your students might like to play with it. The chances are that it was buried for at least twenty-five years."

"Sharyn!" He smiled sardonically. "You think of everything a man could want!"

She stood there, awkwardly, wanting to tell him that she had missed him. The words wouldn't form in her mouth. "It's good that you're back."

"Why? Has there been another murder?"

"No." She shook her head, her face blushing hotly. "I'm, uh, glad to see you. Back. Here. Again." She drew a deep breath. This wasn't going well. "I guess I'll go to the office and get at that paper-work now."

"Stay," he said, taking off his jacket. He ran a hand through his coal black hair that had been streaked with white since he was a teenager. He was too tired to sit around and talk and look at old suitcases. But if it meant she'd stay a little longer...

Two weeks was a long time to spend on the In-ternet, reading the on-line version of the *Gazette,* looking at her picture, as Foster Odom questioned her ability to be the right sheriff for the new millen-nium. He was hungry for her voice and the sparkle in her blue eyes. "Let's take a look at your suitcase. Then I can give it to the kids."

"You just drove back," she protested, looking at his haggard face and tired eyes. "You must be ex-hausted."

"I am," he agreed. "But I can't sleep yet. That's why I came here instead of going to my place."

"All right," she relented. Ernie was right. She *had* missed him. She didn't realize how much until she looked up and saw his face.

"Now, where did you say you got this?" he won-dered as they took the suitcase into the lab.

"It was halfway out of the dirt at the old campground at Bell's Creek," she answered, switching on the overhead lights. "It was probably in the kudzu and brush. I imagine the grader pushed it out into the open when it came through to make room for the buses to park."

"Why are they opening that place again?" he asked, pulling on some latex gloves. "Your father always said that land out there was where Satan walked."

Sharyn frowned. "I don't think it's that bad! There was a murder committed there about twenty-five years ago. It was before my father was sheriff. Grandpa was still running the town with an iron fist back then."

Nick glanced up at her. "A murder seems like a good reason to close the place down. Did they catch who did it?"

"I don't really know," Sharyn admitted. "There's so much said about Bell's Creek: ghosts and demons and shouts for help from the creek at night. I don't remember my father ever talking about it. I'll have to ask Ed. I think Ernie was away in the military when it happened and Joe didn't live here then."

"What about records?"

She shrugged. "There might be some at the old courthouse. I don't think we keep any that old at the office. There's not enough space."

Nick examined the suitcase. "This is a mess.

Whatever's inside is probably full of red clay and rainwater, too."

"The most that would be inside is a child's clothes and a toothbrush."

He ran his hand over the rough sides of the case, stopping when he saw the darker stains on one side. "What's this?"

Sharyn looked at the dark red-brown stains. "More clay and water?"

"Let's see. Get the lights, huh?"

She watched as he sprayed a chemical on the case then held up an ultraviolet light to the stains he'd sprayed. "What is it?"

"Blood," he said. "It's blood."

"It might be from an animal," she suggested.

"Maybe, but look at this." He pointed to a pattern in the material that hadn't been visible without the chemical and light. "This looks like a spray pattern. Maybe arterial spray."

Sharyn thought about the murder. "Maybe this was something from the murder that they didn't find."

"Let's take a look inside," he said, putting the suitcase down on the table again.

She turned on the overhead light. "There was no way to know that the area could be part of a crime scene."

"After twenty-five years and the grader running

through it, there probably wasn't much there anyway." He used a small knife to open the brass lock on the top of the case. It didn't pop open, but Nick coaxed the pieces apart. "It's lined with plastic, the great preserver." Inside the small suitcase were a bloodstained dress, a ring, and a locket. He shook his head. "I wasn't prepared for this. When you bring presents, you like to make them challenging!"

They spent the next hour bagging the contents of the suitcase. Sharyn put on gloves and looked at the dress. It was a pale shade of pink with lace edges and a long skirt. Whoever it belonged to was shorter than her and much smaller. The waist was barely a hand span. It was probably about Kristie's size, she imagined. It was made like the old *Little House on the Prairie* dresses with long sleeves and a high neck.

"This wasn't a child's dress," she said.

"But unless the person had a sick sense of humor, these are puncture wounds." He used a pen to point to the rents in the cloth. "Here. Here. And here."

There was blood surrounding each of the holes. "Should be plenty to type."

"This ring is useless," he said, returning to the other end of the exam table. "It looks like something from the dime store. No, wait, there's a hair trapped in it. That might be useful. But I think this locket is silver, and it's engraved."

"What does it say?" Sharyn asked, holding a pen and paper to write down what he said.

He looked at it under the microscope again. "It's in pretty good shape. There's some blood on it, but I think the initials are EJP." He looked up at her. "EJP. Maybe that was whoever was murdered out there."

"I'll have to check in the morning," she said. "I doubt if any of it was transferred to the computer but there should be some files somewhere."

"It makes my throat feel dry just thinking about the dust." He switched off the light on the microscope. "I can send this stuff off to the state crime lab tonight but that's about all we can do for now. How about some coffee?"

Sharyn glanced at her watch. It was after midnight. "I should go."

Nick rubbed his eyes. "Yeah. It's late. We both have plenty to do tomorrow."

"I guess you came back at just the right time."

"Yeah. I live to serve."

She laughed. "I'll see you tomorrow. Maybe I'll have some answers about that murder."

"It'll be at least twenty-four hours before we hear back on the suitcase and the dress. I think I'll just sleep until then."

"Well, it's good to see you back," she said with a nervous smile. *Too good.*

"It's good to *be* back," he responded. His dark eyes purposefully held hers. "I missed you, Sharyn."

"We all missed you, too."

"Everyone, huh?"

She blinked her wide eyes. Her hand nervously played with the car keys in her pocket. "I missed you, Nick."

"That was tough." He smiled lazily at her. "Good night, Sharyn."

"Aren't you leaving?" she asked.

"In a while."

She nodded. "Good night, Nick."

"SO THE SUITCASE you found at the campground had blood on it?" Kristie asked as she munched on her cereal the next morning.

Sharyn was putting on her badge. "Yes. There was a bloody dress inside of it, too."

"Do you think it belonged to that poor girl who was murdered out there?" Kristie pushed for more information.

"I think that's enough murder talk around the table," Faye Howard told her daughters. She glared at Sharyn. "It's not healthy to eat and talk about dead people at the same time."

"Oh, Mom!"

Sharyn looked at her mother thoughtfully. "You

were here when it happened, Mom. What do you remember about the campground killing?"

"It was a long time ago, Sharyn!"

"I know, but you must have been about my age then."

"I was younger!" her mother informed her tartly. She held her carefully coiffed new hairstyle high on her head.

"But old enough to remember what happened," Kristie agreed with her sister. "What *did* happen out there?"

"Well, I probably wouldn't have known, but I was married to your father at the time. He was already a deputy, working for your grandfather." She shuddered delicately. "It was a terrible thing."

Both daughters watched and waited for her to continue. Faye Howard looked at Sharyn, who was so like T. Raymond with his square jaw and patient eyes. Then she looked at Kristie, who was fair and petite like her. She sighed and continued her ironing.

"Your father told me that one of the girls was found dead in her bunk one morning. Apparently, she'd been stabbed to death during the night while all of the other girls lay sleeping around her. It was the only murder that happened in the county that year. Except for that poor woman who thought her husband was a turkey and slit his throat for Thanksgiving."

Both of the younger women muffled their laughter as Faye pressed her blouse and thought about those times.

"They never found the killer. Your grandfather closed the campground down. He wouldn't let anyone go near it. Even had the road blocked off. The property belonged to the church out there, you know, but the pastor agreed. There was too much evil out there."

"Evil?" Kristie wrinkled her nose. "If people closed down every place there had ever been a murder, most of Chicago and New York, even Charlotte, wouldn't be open to the public."

"And that might be better for everyone!" her mother assured her.

"Here, too. They'd have to close down the sheriff's office and the high school and the convenience store on the corner…" Kristie looked at her mother's shocked face. "Sorry, Mom, but you know what I mean!"

"These conversations can't help but end badly," Faye said, her throat full of emotion as she thought about the convenience store where T. Raymond had been shot and killed. It was less than a mile from their house. She passed it every day since then. But she'd never gone inside again. "My mother had the right idea. It's best for ladies not to talk about such things!"

"Ladies!" Kristie snorted. "Sharyn is the sheriff. I don't think she qualifies as a *lady!*"

Faye looked at her older daughter in her terrible brown uniform. "You might be right, dear. But it's what's *inside* the uniform that counts."

"I have to go," Sharyn said, stifling the urge to strangle her mother. "I'm going to try to find the files that go with that suitcase."

"I'll be at the campground all day," Kristie told them. "Only a week before we open and the buses start rolling in! I want to thank you both for all of your help."

"Don't forget to thank Caison, too, honey."

"I would, but he would use it for his own political agenda."

"Your sister might be running again, too, you know," her mother retorted, annoyed. "Since she didn't make it to my engagement party to make the announcement about *not* running, I guess we won't know until the election."

"Don't start, Mom," Sharyn advised. "You know why I couldn't come that night."

"I know, Sharyn. And it's the same reason I asked you *not* to run!"

"Because you don't want her to die in a stock car accident like Trudy's husband?" Kristie asked with deep irreverence.

"I'm leaving," Sharyn said, getting out the door

before her mother could reply to her sister's usual jab at anything that smacked of establishment. "I'll probably be late tonight."

"You always are." Faye Howard sighed. "Just like your father."

"That doesn't mean she'll die like Dad!" Kristie added fuel to her already callous remarks.

Sharyn closed the door to the house before she could hear her mother's reply. She climbed into her Jeep and was about to leave when she saw a man hammering a sign into her front yard. The street was already filled with campaign signs that were blue, red, and white, announcing different candidates for different offices.

This sign was the bright blue one she recognized as Roy Tarnower's. It had a picture of him and the words, EXPERIENCED and BOUND TO DUTY. Roy had been the sheriff for one term between her grandfather and her father. He had been running against her father the year T. Raymond had died and had filed a complaint when Sharyn was elected to office. He'd made it very clear what he thought about the sheriff's daughter running for office in her father's place.

Sharyn rolled down her window. "Good morning, Mr. Daggott."

The man glanced up. "Morning, Sharyn." He continued pounding the sign into the ground. He was hitting it so hard that he was shaking the dogwood petals off the tree close to him.

"What are you doing, Mr. Daggott?"

"I'm putting up a campaign sign. Your mama said it would be okay."

"Does she know what signs you're putting up?" Sharyn wondered.

He nodded. "I told her that I was putting up a sign for Roy for sheriff and a sign for Senator Talbot."

"That's crossing party lines, Mr. Daggott," she reminded him.

He stopped pounding and stood back to look at the sign firmly planted in the damp spring ground. "Any law against that, Sheriff?"

She smiled. "None that I know of, sir."

"Good. Otherwise I'd have to start my own campaign against government interference!" He laughed and walked up to her Jeep. "Why aren't you running for sheriff again, Sharyn?"

"I didn't say I wasn't."

He glanced at the sign in the ground. "Your mama voting for the opposition?"

"Maybe she misunderstood," Sharyn told him.

"You run," he told her. "I'll vote for you. You're young but you've done a good job so far. Not your fault Diamond Springs is changing."

"Thanks, Mr. Daggott. I'll let you know."

"Better do that," he answered. "And quick!"

"I will, sir. Thank you."

"I'm going to have a talk with your mama!"

Sharyn looked at Ray Tarnower's sign again, then pulled out of the driveway. She was waiting longer than most to make up her mind. The party manager had told her the same thing, often and loudly. In all fairness to them, she would have to make a decision soon. She put the thought behind her and drove to the office.

She missed seeing Charlie's welcoming face at the gate to the back parking lot at the sheriff's office. He'd been there as a deputy for forty years before he took partial retirement, and then worked in the lot for another five. He knew all the old stories. He would have been the person to ask about the killing out at the campground, but he was too ill.

With Charlie gone, they'd installed a new surveillance camera and there was a guard dog on duty at night after the place was locked up. It made Ernie feel safer, but Sharyn liked it better the old way. If she didn't know Ernie better, she'd think that he *wanted* Charlie to retire. He'd had a fit when Foster Odom had sneaked in a few months back. But that wouldn't be like Ernie. Even though he'd changed since he'd been living with Annie, his high school sweetheart, and the ordeal of being accused of murder, he was still Ernie.

He met her at the back door, his uniform pressed straight and his only sprig of hair flat back on his head. He had a cup of coffee in one hand and a notebook in the other. "Morning, Sheriff."

"Good morning, Ernie."

"You have a meeting with the county commission this Wednesday at ten. They want to talk about those salary increases you asked for last month. Nick is on the phone about the blood in the suitcase. I checked the files in the computer, but there's no mention of the killing at the campground. It doesn't go back that far."

Sharyn took her coffee from him, no longer surprised that he knew what they would be working on that day without her telling him. "Thanks."

"And I have these for you to sign." He handed her the clipboard as they walked to her office. One paper was a simple requisition form to have work done on one of the sheriff's cars. But the other was a candidate's form from the local party headquarters. It was all filled out, except for her signature.

She looked at him as she hung up her coat. "Did you think I wouldn't notice?"

He shrugged. "You don't always look at everything you sign."

"Ernie! I can't believe you thought you could trick me into running for sheriff."

"It's for your own good!"

"I'm going to decide." She handed him the paper, unsigned.

"When?"

"Soon."

"Sheriff—"

"Let me take Nick's call, Ernie. Then we can talk."

He sat in a chair close to her father's big old desk and looked up at the pictures of old Jacob and T. Raymond scowling down at him. *I tried,* he explained to them silently. *But she's as stubborn as both of you were!*

"I've only got a minute before I go to sleep for the next twenty-four hours," Nick told her when she picked up the phone.

"You've been up all night?"

"Don't complain! I have a blood type for you and I can tell you that the blood *on* the suitcase matches the blood *in* the suitcase. They're both human blood, type A. The pattern I was telling you about on the case is consistent with one of the stab wounds in the dress. Without the body, I can't say for sure what it was that stabbed her. The rest will have to come from the lab. Good night." He hung up before she could speak again.

Sharyn put down the phone and looked at Ernie. "Nick says it was human blood on the suitcase."

Ernie nodded. "Then let's get to work."

She stood up. Ernie didn't move.

"Aren't we going to get to work? The files have to be across the street in the old courthouse."

"You aren't still going on about your mama asking you not to run for sheriff, are you?" He shook his head. "I think she means well, but you know Faye says things sometimes that aren't right."

Sharyn had grown up calling this man Uncle Ernie. He was as close to family, without having the same blood, as he could be. He had supported her in running for sheriff after her father had been killed. He had helped her with the job for the first awkward years when all of the other deputies were resentful and angry. She felt she owed him an explanation.

"Let's talk on the way to the old courthouse," she said, swallowing the last of her coffee. "How's Annie doing today?"

They walked out of her office together. It was strange not to have Trudy there at the front desk, answering phones and yelling out messages and other instructions. She hadn't come back to work after her husband's fiery death in a stock car accident. She and Ben had been married for almost thirty years and had four children together. Sharyn understood, but she was hard to replace. They had gone through three temps in as many months.

"Annie's okay," Ernie replied. "She's with her

mama today. Since her daddy died, her mama talks about Billy Bost all the time. Drives Annie crazy!"

They walked past the front desk but there was no sign of their temp. There was only a short note detailing why she wasn't coming back again.

Ernie sighed and took out his cell phone. "I'll call the temp agency."

Sharyn asked a volunteer to answer the phones. The other deputies were either out on patrol or answering 911 calls. They really needed at least five more deputies, but the chances of her getting them before the elections weren't good. After the elections, the new sheriff and commission members would wrangle over the budget.

The new sheriff. She realized the bend of her thoughts as Ernie was putting away his cell phone and they were ready to cross the street.

"They're sending someone else over," Ernie told her. "But this is our last temp from them."

"Why?"

He shrugged and pocketed his phone. "They said we're too hard to work for. The last one said she was too nervous to get up in the morning."

"She didn't even work through a murder investigation," Sharyn remarked.

"Yeah. She was lucky. But that man *did* come in last week with a 'possum in his shirt."

Sharyn smiled. "You mean the one who wanted to file charges against those boys for teasing the 'possum?"

"That's the one. Maybe you just don't appreciate the stress of the job." He glanced at her from the corner of his eye. "Or maybe you do. Is that why you aren't running for re-election?"

"Ernie—"

"You know I'm not letting this rest until I understand what's going on, Sheriff."

They had reached the old courthouse. It had been built in 1809 and had stood through fierce storms, spring flooding, and deep snow blowing down from the mountains. It had been renovated in the last few years. The spire on the roof, not unlike a church spire, had a shiny gold patina and there were green shutters on the windows. The bell was electric now but it pealed every day at lunchtime. The building was only used now for storage or the occasional special city promotion. Otherwise, it sat silent and empty on the corner across from the new pink granite courthouse.

Sharyn put her key into the ornate brass lock as a formation of Canadian geese flew by overhead. The cherry tree outside the old courthouse had already lost its flowers in the last heavy frost that had marked the end of winter, but some cheerful tulips were blooming and a few sweet yellow bells were dancing in the breeze from Diamond Lake.

"Sheriff?"

"Ernie," she said as she opened the door. "The truth is that I'm just not sure. I keep going over it in my mind. I'm the sheriff. I think I'm a good sheriff. But if my father hadn't died, I wouldn't have challenged him for the position. I would've been a lawyer and I think I would've been happy there, too."

"That sounds like Faye's thinking," Ernie remarked, following her into the musty old building. He locked the door behind them. "You didn't kill your daddy to become sheriff. It happened. You can't change what's past. You've been a good sheriff. You could help this town grow. You know it's gonna need help. What do you think old Roy Tarnower is gonna do if he wins? It'll be back to business as usual. The good old boys taking the town back from that young upstart sheriff."

Sharyn smiled. "Am I a young upstart?"

"Compared to Roy and Judge Hamilton and Jack Winter, yes, ma'am. You are a young upstart who isn't willing to look the other way and won't let them get away with their shenanigans."

"Shenanigans?" she asked, wandering into the records area where the old documents were kept.

"You know what I mean," he growled at her. "I

wish your daddy was alive right now to whip some sense into you!"

"We've gone over that, Ernie," she replied calmly. "If he were alive, I wouldn't be here right now. I might be defending Donald Richmond's murderer."

"This is getting us nowhere."

Sharyn put her hand on his arm. Ernie was small but he was whipcord strong. She'd seen him handle men twice his size without losing his breath. She really felt she should be persuading him to run for sheriff in her place. But he'd made it clear to her that he wasn't interested because of his new relationship with Annie and because of the politics that he hated. That's why he hadn't run for sheriff when her father had been killed, even though, as lead deputy, he would've been the logical replacement.

That was her problem, she decided. She couldn't give anyone a *good* reason why she shouldn't run. She was just having some doubts and wanted to think it through before she committed again.

"Ernie, like you're always reminding me, you've known me since I was a baby."

"And changed some of your diapers!"

"We won't go there!" she laughed. "You know I need time to think it over. I'm not the kind of person who jumps into things, especially four-year terms in office, battling the commissioners and Jack Winter and Nick—"

"Don't go there either," he warned, squeezing her hand on his arm. "Not unless you want to hear a bucket full of truth!"

"Ernie!"

"I know what you're trying to say, Sharyn. I just don't think you ever thought about it this way until Faye had that little talk with you."

"Whether you like it or not," Sharyn said, turning to go into the records room, "whether *I* like it or not, she's my mother! I appreciate you trying to look out for me but I have to decide this on my own. And I'm still deciding. I haven't decided *not* to run yet."

"Okay." He shrugged. "Let's look for those records."

Nick had been right about the dust and the cobwebs. People didn't come to look up anything much at the courthouse. Apparently, no one *ever* came to clean. The old sheriff's records were kept in a single room. It made it easier not to have to sort through all the official records of the whole town.

"Have you noticed Jack Winter is running unopposed for D.A.?" Ernie asked as they looked through the old files.

"Who would run against him?"

"I went to a rally last month for a lawyer from

one of the new housing developments. He was thinking about running."

"What happened to him?" she asked.

"He suddenly decided not to run when his house caught on fire. He moved back to Charlotte."

Sharyn paused in her reading. "How many things can Jack Winter get away with without getting caught?"

"Did you see or hear anything about this man filing charges against him or asking for an inquest?"

"No."

Ernie nodded. "There you go. He can get away with it as long as people are too scared to face him."

She frowned. "Or can't prove anything against him?"

"I know what you're gonna say, and you might as well not bother! We checked and double-checked, Sheriff. We all feel that Jack Winter was responsible for Trudy's husband getting killed but we can't prove it. Had he ever been near the raceway? No. He claimed he didn't even know Ben but it was as clear as water that he was involved. Ben challenged him on those horses he had taken away from him for cruelty. The D.A. wasn't gonna forget that."

"It leaves me with a bad taste in my mouth," Sharyn admitted. "I want to take Jack Winter down. The man thinks we're all his personal puppets. He sits in that big office and pulls the strings and we all dance."

Ernie squinted up at her through the fragmented sun motes that came in through the cracks in the shutters. "And you want motivation to run for sheriff?"

"Nick told me I could beat Jack Winter, but not up front. In that case, I couldn't exactly run on a ticket for cleaning up corruption."

"Nick knows what he's talking about," Ernie replied. "I would've said the same— Hold on! I found it!"

"What?"

"The file with the information from the campground murder. It's kind of weird thinking about old Jacob putting this together for us to look at all these years later."

"Kind of makes you not mind doing the paperwork as much, huh?"

He shook his head. Sharyn closed the drawer she'd had open. "Nah."

They took the file to the small wooden table pushed into one corner of the room. The old pages were yellowed at the edges. Mistakes were crossed out and re-written by hand on the typewritten material. There were lists of everything, except suspects. The whole account was laid out in painstaking detail but there was no resolution. The case file was marked *unsolved*.

"No one was ever arrested for this," Ernie remarked, glancing through the papers slowly.

"They didn't do much paperwork back then, did they?"

"Things change," Ernie said. "But where are your granddaddy's remarks and observations? I know he made some. There's not enough here to find someone who forgot to pay a speeding ticket."

"There's this," Sharyn pointed out to him. "The murdered girl's name was Rebecca Liston. She lived in Frog Meadow. She was a student at the elementary school there. She was stabbed to death in her bunk at the campground while the other girls slept around her. But she's not the murder victim we're looking for."

"Why not?"

"To begin with, her initials are wrong. The locket was inscribed *EJP*. Her initials were RAL. They don't have a lot on her forensics but they do have a blood type. Nick said the other girl's blood type was A. Rebecca's was O positive."

Ernie shook his head. "Here we go again."

THREE

THE FOG HADN'T LIFTED from the ground yet when Sharyn pulled into the old campground the following morning. It lay like a shroud, hiding some of the cabins, obscuring others. It was still cold and damp in the mornings, even though the days were warm and sunny. She shrugged on her brown jacket over her uniform and stepped out of her Jeep.

She'd spent most of the day before looking through the old records. There had only been the one report on Rebecca Liston's death, poorly detailed as it was. Ernie was right. There wasn't enough to find anything. The blood work and basic observations about the body were all the coroner had added. The coroner, at the time of the murder, had also been the local funeral director. He'd looked at her while he got her ready for burial and recorded what he'd seen.

Rebecca had been twelve years old. She'd died of five stab wounds, two striking the heart. Essentially, the coroner had found that she'd bled to death in her bed with possible help all around her.

The killer had sneaked into the cabin, ignored the five other girls sleeping there, and chosen her to kill. There were no entries in the record about possible reasons why that had happened. Just the facts.

Sharyn walked through the swirling gray mist to cabin number five. It was strange that everyone recalled it so vividly, yet no one had known for sure which cabin was the murder scene. She'd only known from the report her grandfather had written. From her place in the campground, Sharyn couldn't see any of the other cabins around her. The sounds were muffled by the road and the trees.

Cabin number five hadn't been restored. It was one of those that the county had declared unsound. The front door was open but there was only a wall behind it. The entrance was to the side, beside a set of stairs that ran up to the roof on the outside. There were also two fake windows that faced the front. The rest of the windows were real.

Sharyn pushed away the yellow tape that declared it UNSAFE and stepped inside, out of the fog. The cabin was coarsely made. She guessed that a hundred years ago when they were built, people weren't as worried about their kids getting splinters in their fingers. The floor, walls, and ceiling were made of rough-hewn boards. The cabin was empty now. There would have been six beds in that single room when Rebecca was murdered. At the back of the room was a staircase that led to the ceiling and ended there. There was no upstairs.

She shook her head, not understanding why people had thought that something like that would keep the devil away. From all the stories she'd heard about the devil in the Uwharries, he was pretty tricky. She didn't think fake doors and misleading stairways would stop him.

She didn't believe the old tales of ghosts and demons and ghost trains rumbling through the night, but the camp definitely had an air of remorse about it. Swallowed in the drifting white fog, it seemed remote and isolated from the rest of the world. She could understand why people imagined hearing screams from the nearby creek where thirty people had drowned before the camp was built.

Sharyn read through the report that involved the cabin again. It named all of the little girls that slept in the room that night. A crude sketch showed the positions of the six beds. Rebecca had slept in the bed near the stairway that went into the ceiling. The front door and windows had been barred from the inside because they'd been afraid of bears.

She went up the stairs carefully and pushed at the boards in the ceiling but nothing moved. There were no cut marks in the wood. The stairway wasn't real. There didn't appear to be any change in what her grandfather had seen twenty-five years ago. In a room, barred from the inside, a girl, surrounded by other girls and a counselor, had been killed in her sleep. Someone had picked her out of that group and stabbed her to death.

She turned to start back down the stairs and almost jumped out of her skin. There was a man at the foot of the stairs, looking up at her.

"Sheriff Howard."

"Yes." She recovered herself without falling down the stairs. "I'm Sharyn Howard." She put out her hand.

"Pastor Paul Reynolds." The man extended his hand to her. He was dressed all in black and carried a well-worn black bible in his left hand. He shook her hand but there was no welcoming expression on his face.

"You're Keith's father," Sharyn surmised. "Kristie is my sister."

"I'm aware of that, Sheriff."

"You must be very proud of Keith."

"Must I?" Paul Reynolds glanced around the empty cabin. "I wish we'd had this place leveled years ago so it couldn't be re-opened. No good can come of it."

"Mr. Reynolds, I think the children that come here will disagree. If you're talking about the murder that happened here, the camp was open a hundred years before that unfortunate tragedy. Nothing happened before then."

"Easy to be smug when you don't live in the devil's backyard, Sheriff."

Sharyn stared at the obviously agitated man. "Is there a problem, sir? Is there something that I should know about? You can talk to me."

"You should know better than to let people meddle where they aren't wanted or needed, Sheriff! I'm asking you to stop this before it's too late!"

"Do you have information about the murder, Mr. Reynolds?"

"No, of course not! I just know this area. I grew up here. It's hard enough for locals to live here. We don't need outsiders!"

"That murder was a long time ago," Sharyn told him softly. "We don't have a lot of information about it. But we did find a suitcase, half-buried in the dirt out there. Any idea where it could have come from?"

"Twenty-five years ago when this murder happened, I was in seminary school in Raleigh," the pastor told her through tightly clenched teeth. "I wouldn't know."

"I appreciate your help, sir," Sharyn said, taking out a card. "If you can think of anything else, please let me know."

The pastor glared at her. His brown eyes were

anguished in his thin face. "For the sake of everyone, I want you to close this down, Sheriff! I've spoken with Keith but he's too crazy about your sister to listen to me!"

She ignored the jibe about her sister. "Doesn't the campground still belong to the church, sir? Couldn't you close it down?"

"Not anymore, Sheriff. Jacob Howard made the church deed the land to the county so that it couldn't be re-opened. I guess he didn't think about his own granddaughter being so stubborn that she couldn't see the darkness coming!"

"Sir, I—"

"Do what you have to do, Sheriff! I'll do what I must do!"

Sharyn watched him storm out of the cabin. She glanced around the dismal room and followed him out, closing the door behind her. The pastor had already disappeared into the fog. She walked back to the front of the campground where a team of workers was getting ready to lay gravel on the bus parking area. She knew the chances were that there was nothing left behind that would make a difference, but she had them put the procedure off for another day.

Something terrible had happened at Bell's Creek campground but it didn't have anything to do with the devil. This was the work of an ordinary human.

Kristie wanted to have her first campers arriving in a week. Sharyn wanted to make sure it was safe. It was beginning to look as though there had been two murders that had gone unsolved.

She thought about Keith's father on the way back to the office. Paul Reynolds was scared. He was a colorless man, his hair almost matching his eyes. His face was pale and his lips were thin with worry. This wasn't a man who was happy with his life.

Maybe he saw too much of the darker side to be happy anymore. She supposed pastors did hear and see terrible things.

Keith didn't seem to be like him, except for a slightly serious bent to his personality. Kristie was so outgoing and cheerful, it was hard to imagine her fitting into that family. It had to be a case of opposites attracting! Kristie, a blond ex-cheerleader who wanted to be a pediatrician, was dating Keith, who wanted to be a medical examiner and was the son of a dark pastor. Sharyn shuddered.

She parked out on the street in front of the office. She planned on going out later when she had more information. Nick had left a message that the information was back about the suitcase and its contents. Maybe that would provide a few more answers.

The office seemed empty when she walked inside. Usually, deputies, volunteers, and highway patrol officers were littering the place, talking on the phones and shuffling reports. The phone rang but no one answered. Sharyn took a deep breath. It was going to be another day without someone to answer the phones. Ernie must not have been successful with the temp service.

Someone picked up the phone. "Line two, Sheriff," she sang out. "It's your mother."

Sharyn rounded the corner and saw Trudy at her desk. All of the deputies were staggered around her. David and J.P. looked haggard after being out on patrol all night but they were smiling and talking with Trudy. "You're back!"

"Couldn't stay gone forever," Trudy said with some of her old gusto. "You've gone and hired someone else while I was out, I see." She glanced at J.P. "Anything else I need to know?"

"How much we missed you!" Ed told her, giving her a squeeze that lifted her up out of her chair.

"Put me down, Deputy!" Trudy commanded. "I don't think we like that kind of behavior in this office!"

"Tell my mother I'll call her," Sharyn told her. "I'm glad you're back, Trudy. You don't know how much we've missed you."

"I don't know how you keep this office straight," Ernie added. "We've gone through so many temps that the service said we couldn't have another!"

"That's 'cause Ed hits on them all," Joe replied

with a laugh. "They leave to get away from his ugly face!"

Ed glared at his partner. "You're just jealous."

"Okay, settle down," Trudy told them. "I know why you couldn't keep anyone. It's because you have to be crazy to be here. The sheriff and I have talked about it before."

"She's right," Sharyn agreed, picking up her mail. "But I'm glad you're still crazy, Trudy. Thanks for coming back."

Trudy's familiar face was a little sadder, a little thinner since Ben had died. Her smile wasn't as bright. Sharyn guessed it wouldn't ever be the same again. Trudy and Ben had been married a long time. They had been devoted to each other. His death had devastated her.

"Could I talk to you a minute, Sheriff?" David asked, fingering his thick brown mustache.

"Ed's taking patrol," Joe told her. "What's up with this campground thing?"

"Don't leave yet, Ed," Sharyn said quickly.

"Conference room," Ernie said, following her lead. "Where's Nick?"

"I don't know. I had a message from him."

"I'll give him a call," Ernie offered.

"David, in my office," Sharyn agreed. "J.P., go home. You look exhausted."

"Thanks," the other deputy said. "See you tomorrow, David."

"Yeah," David agreed, then followed Sharyn into her office.

"What is it, David?" she asked him, hoping it was something legitimate. With David, she could never be sure. It probably had something to do with a woman.

"It's about Cari, Assistant Deputy Long."

"What about her?" Sharyn sighed, knowing the two had been seeing each other.

"I was wondering if she could be assigned to nights so we could be together more. It's hard with me working at night and her working days."

"Did Cari ask you to do this?" Sharyn asked.

"No. I just thought—"

"No."

He stopped and smiled. "What?"

"I said no. She can't be re-assigned. I want her here during the day to train. She's only working four hours."

"As a deputy trainee," David argued. "She's still working four hours on the computer research."

"Sorry, David. The only way I can justify training another sheriff's deputy right now is because she's already working here on the computers. I need her here during the day. If this is a hardship for her—"

"This *is* a hardship for her," he replied. "She can't see *me* very often."

Sharyn smiled at him. "Is that a hardship for her or for you?"

"Both!"

"No."

"But you just said—"

"Go home, David. Get some sleep. Cari stays where she is. You'll have to work out the details of your romance for yourselves."

"It's just because you don't have a life!"

"David—"

"It's true! You live and breathe this place and you think everyone else should, too!"

"That's why I'm the sheriff, David! Now go home!"

David scowled but he didn't say anything else. He walked out of the office. Sharyn followed him out and went to the conference room that doubled as the interrogation room. Cari was there at the banged-up old wooden table. She looked up, and then looked away quickly.

"All right. Maybe we can get started. Where's Nick?"

"Not at his office," Ernie told her. "And not at his apartment."

"You know how Nick can be," Ed said. "He's probably just being difficult."

Sharyn shrugged, annoyed, but not willing to show it. "Never mind. We have enough to get started with anyway."

"Are we gonna investigate the old campground killing?" Ed asked.

"That's why I asked you to stay," she nodded. "What do you remember about it, Ed?"

He glanced around at everyone at the table. "Am I the only one who remembers it?"

"I was in Philly then," Joe explained.

"And I was in the army," Ernie added. "I came back just after it was over."

"I, uh, looked up what I could find about it in the *Gazette*," Cari interjected in a very quiet voice.

"Great," Sharyn praised her. "Did you make copies?"

"Yes," she agreed, standing up to hand out the copies of the old newspaper account.

"This is what I recall about it, Sheriff," Ed explained after reading the newspaper account. "I didn't pay much attention. I was dating this widow. She was twice as old as me at the time but she was—" He looked up and saw the rest of the group looking at him. "Never mind. But I remember what this says. There was a little girl killed out at the campground. I remember people talking about the old ghost stories from Bell's Creek."

"My mother wrote to me about it," Ernie recalled. "She said Bell's Creek was a bad place and they shouldn't have had children out there anyway."

"Well, this is what we found yesterday." Sharyn handed out copies of the records she and Ernie had dug up. "It's not much. But what we have now is a suitcase with a girl's dress in it. The dress was covered with blood and had tears in it that Nick identified as puncture wounds to vital organs. The suitcase was covered in blood, part of which was an arterial spray pattern that would be consistent with one of those wounds. It was human blood, type A."

"The killer must have left it behind," Joe conjectured.

"That would be nice, but Rebecca Anne Liston's blood was type O positive. She was found, still in her nightgown, in the cabin. And believe it or not, from her height and weight, she was probably too big to wear the dress in the suitcase. This belonged to a short, slender girl, maybe five-one or five-two, probably not more than ninety to one hundred pounds. Rebecca was a little chubby and taller. There was also a silver locket in the suitcase with the initials EJP inscribed on it. Obviously not Rebecca Anne Liston's initials. Also the hair color. Rebecca was dark-haired. There was blond hair found wrapped around a ring in the suitcase.

"So another girl died out there that no one knew about?"

Sharyn sighed. "I think so."

"Is it possible that the dress in the suitcase belonged to the killer?" Cari asked.

"I thought about that," Sharyn agreed. "I had hoped to ask Nick that question today."

"You mean one little girl killed another little girl?" Ed asked in disbelief.

"I hope not," Sharyn replied. "Ed, you're on patrol today. Ernie, you could look up the names of the other girls in the cabin with Rebecca and we'll see if any of them still live around here. I'd like to hear their account. I looked it up and Rebecca's parents still live in the same house in Frog Meadow. We're going out to see them today."

"What about me, Sheriff?" Cari asked.

"I can't let you go out yet, Cari," Sharyn apologized. "But I can let you do some computer work. Get me any other info you can about the camp. Counselors, financial backing, whatever you can find. Also, check out the state buying or taking that land from the Bell's Creek church after the murder."

"Thanks, Sheriff! I'll get right on it!"

"Thank you, Cari."

"And, Sheriff? About that thing with David—"

"Never mind, Cari," Sharyn told her, realizing the wall between her office and the conference room was pretty thin. "I'll handle David."

"I'll have a word with him, Sheriff," Ed offered.

"I'll take care of it, Ed. I have to deal with David." She glanced meaningfully at Ernie, who looked away. Ernie had intervened between Sharyn and David before.

"Okay." He shrugged his broad shoulders beneath his white uniform shirt. "What do you want me to do, then?"

"As soon as Ernie pulls up those names, he'll send some of them to you. I'd like you to go out and start talking with those children. We'll take the rest."

"They probably aren't kids anymore, Sheriff," Joe added.

"I know. Take your time. Their recall is bound to be fuzzy. Let me know if any of them say anything different than what we already know."

"Okay."

"Well?" Ernie wondered. "Am I driving?"

"No, you're riding. Bring your laptop," she answered.

"What about Nick?" he asked.

"We'll call him later. He's bound to turn up."

The Listons' home was a small, yellow clapboard house with a metal roof. It struck Sharyn as ironic that the house was almost the same color as the cabin where their daughter had been found dead. Had they painted it that color on purpose? She knew people did strange things to remember their loved ones.

Jolie and Harris Liston were both at home. They worked nights in a local T-shirt factory. They welcomed Sharyn and Ernie into their small home. Jolie went to make coffee while Harris smoothed out the wrinkles in the sofa throw cover.

"I know it's been a long time," Sharyn said after she had explained why they were there that day. "And I apologize for having to bring it up again. But we thought you might know some details that were left out of the original report."

"Having our daughter die was the hardest thing that ever came through our lives," Harris told her with a shake of his graying head.

"Rebecca was our only child. We didn't have any more," Jolie explained, handing Sharyn and Ernie each a cup of coffee. "We didn't want any more. She was so bright and happy. All of her short life."

"I know how hard this must be for you," Sharyn began.

"You can't know, Sheriff," Harris insisted. "Seeing her there like that. Knowing someone had done that to her."

Sharyn bowed her head. The parents' grief was

still so strong that it was tangible. "You're right, sir. I don't know what it's like to lose a child to violence but I know how hard it was to go into that store after they'd shot my father. I identified his body."

"That's right." Jolie looked at Harris. "I forgot you lost kin to violence, too, Sheriff. It's hard either way. I'm sure you didn't love your father any less than we loved our Rebecca. What do you need to know?"

"Did the sheriff have any idea who did this to your daughter?"

"That was your granddaddy wasn't it, Sheriff Howard?" Harris asked.

"Yes, sir, it was."

"He was a good man." He shook his head. "He tried hard to find Rebecca's killer but no one could ever find any reason for it. They talked with the people at school. They talked with her friends. They checked out people here in town. There never was anyone who might be a suspect."

"Did they ever think it could have been one of the girls in the cabin with her?" Ernie asked quietly.

Jolie Liston caught her breath. "What are you saying?"

"We just wanted to know if they questioned the other girls," Sharyn replied.

"They questioned everybody, Sheriff. There was no one to blame for her death but that foul place!

How did someone get in there and kill her without waking any of the rest of them? Why did the devil pick our Rebecca? Because that's who did it, Sheriff. The devil. Everyone knows he lives in Bell's Creek. He kept our angel there with him!"

Sharyn and Ernie left soon after the emotional outburst. The Listons saw them politely to their car.

"We brought all that back up for nothing," Ernie said as they left the Liston house. "Those poor people."

"I guess it's something you never get over," Sharyn answered as they got back in the Jeep. "I don't think anyone has ever questioned the other girls in the cabin, Ernie. You saw the look on their faces when you mentioned it. I don't believe the other girls were involved either but they might have seen something and not realized it."

"You don't believe or don't *want* to believe?"

"You choose. It seems like a possible answer, since there's no report of another girl missing at the campground. They closed it down right after the murder. Yet here's this suitcase with a bloody dress in it. None of the other girls heard or saw anything that night."

"There are only three of the five girls left around here. I sent their names to Joe. One of the girls is dead. She died from breast cancer last year. Another girl is living in Wyoming."

"Which leaves us going back to town to see what Cari dug up. Maybe Nick can tell us what else he got back on the suitcase."

"That's about it," he agreed. He was looking through the report. "I don't see much more than a cursory questioning of the counselors at the campground. Jacob must have felt like they weren't involved. Did you know your Aunt Selma was a counselor there?"

"Really?" Sharyn asked, following the road back to Diamond Springs. "I didn't know that. I wonder what she remembers. I was at the campground this morning."

"Alone?"

"Ernie, there isn't anything evil about the campground."

"That may be true," he argued. "But that doesn't make it safe for you to be out there alone."

Sharyn shrugged it off. "I ran into Keith's father, Paul Reynolds. He's kind of spooky. He was upset. Maybe a little afraid. He told me the campground shouldn't be reopened and that Keith was too infatuated with Kristie to see it."

"You think he might be involved in some way?"

"I don't see his name mentioned on any of the reports. He told me he was at seminary school in Raleigh when the murder happened. I know the church owned the campground until the murder.

I don't know. It was like he came to out there especially to find me. He talked about evil but he looked like a man who was afraid of something much more real."

"He's a church pastor, Sheriff," Ernie acknowledged. "Evil is pretty real to him."

"Maybe we should pay him a visit. See what you make of him," she suggested.

"Okay. Can't hurt. Easy enough to check if he was telling the truth about Raleigh. Although I can't imagine his motive for killing that little girl."

"Who could have any motive, besides insanity, to kill a twelve-year-old girl?" Sharyn questioned.

He shook his head. "That's true enough."

Sharyn called the office. Joe was back from interviewing two of the three girls still living in the area. The third girl was on vacation and couldn't be reached. The first two didn't remember much more than Ed about the whole thing.

"They couldn't even recall the dead girl's name," Joe told Sharyn. "I've got a call from Harmony. Seems there's a cow wandering through the downtown area. I sure am glad they did away with animal control and let us do those jobs."

"Head on over," Sharyn said with a laugh. "See if you can find out who owns it. Don't try to catch it yourself."

"Can I shoot it?"

"No! Not unless it's vicious or something."

"All right. I'll let you know." He hung up the phone.

"What's up?" Ernie asked.

"A cow is loose in downtown Harmony. Without animal control, that leaves Joe rounding it up."

Ernie smiled. "Cows can be vicious. I had an uncle that was attacked by one. Bit him in the leg."

"A cow?"

"Yeah. He had cold hands when he went to milk her and she took exception to it."

Sharyn laughed, putting on her turn signal to slide into the driveway of the parsonage at Bell's Creek Church. "Well, maybe Joe won't try to milk her."

"Joe wouldn't know which end to milk!"

Sharyn took a deep breath. "He's right, though. We can't go around chasing stray animals. There are too many other things to do. The county has to reinstate animal control."

"They're not likely to do that until after the election," he said.

"I know."

"And you probably won't care by then."

"Why not?"

He smiled at her with his Ernie half-smile. "Because Roy Tarnower is gonna be the next sheriff and all you'll have to do is worry about saving his arrests from going to jail."

"Ernie!"

"All right! All right!" He put his hands up to surrender. "You don't want to talk about it. It's not your twenty-year pension."

"You're saying you'll lose your job if Roy takes over?"

"Nope. I'm saying I'll *quit* my job." He closed the Jeep door.

"No pressure or anything to make up my mind, huh?"

He shrugged. "If Faye can exert her influence—"

"You really aren't my father, you know." She smiled at him.

"Most of the time I feel like I should be. Somebody's got to keep you straight, young lady!"

Sharyn laughed. It was what her father used to say to her. "I haven't heard that in a long time."

"I know." He patted her shoulder. "It felt good to say it. Let's go and find your spooky pastor."

They rang the bell at the old parsonage door. It was a big, squat two-story house built more for space than for beauty. The front door and the two front windows made the house appear as if it had a face that looked out on the church across the gravel road. The porch was slightly weather-beaten and needed a good coat of paint. A few small purple crocuses were peeking through the brown dirt and old leaves on the ground. There was a plaque on the red brick that proclaimed that the house had been built in 1907.

"Yes?" An older man answered the door. He looked at Sharyn and Ernie with a wary eye.

"Sheriff Sharyn Howard, sir. This is Deputy Ernie Watkins. We're looking for Paul Reynolds."

The old man nodded his gray head. "What's he done now?"

Sharyn glanced at Ernie. "Has he been in trouble before, sir?"

"That boy's middle name is trouble, Sheriff! Come on in and sit a spell. He should be home soon and you can talk to him."

The parsonage was dark on the inside, with few windows to bring in any natural light and only a few small lamps. There was a cluttered piano on one wall and a stack of church magazines on the floor. The carpet underfoot was worn. The furniture looked as though it had been there since the house had been built.

"Coffee?" the old man asked them.

"Thank you, sir," Ernie jumped in. "That old weather's still got a nip to it."

"Yes, it does, Deputy."

"Are you Paul's father, sir?" he guessed.

"Yes." He looked around the room. "I was the

pastor here myself for forty years. Ezekiel Reynolds." He put out his hand to Ernie.

"Nice to meet you, sir," Ernie reciprocated.

Ezekiel Reynolds gave his hand to Sharyn. He looked like he was as old as the house, too, she thought. He was tall and gaunt, with his son's worried brown eyes. But his handshake was strong to the point of being painful.

"I'll just get that coffee," he told them with a smile.

"Thank you, sir," Sharyn responded.

"I wonder which of them was the pastor here when the murder happened," Ernie said when the man had disappeared down a dark hallway.

"Paul told me he was in seminary school," Sharyn confided. "Maybe we should be in the kitchen, talking to his father."

They walked down the dark hall to the well-lit kitchen. The room had an old-fashioned air about it, offset by a few modern appliances. Ezekiel was standing at the coffee maker, carefully measuring coffee into the upper chamber.

"Sorry it takes so long, but my hands aren't as sure as they once were," he told them.

"We came back here to talk to you, Mr. Reynolds," Ernie said. "You must have been the pastor here about the time of that murder at the campground."

Ezekiel turned to him. "Murder?" His long face grew angry. "At *our* campground?"

Sharyn smiled at him. "You don't remember the little girl being killed at the campground, sir?"

His eyes cleared. "Oh, yes. Of course. What a shame that was! The devil was there that night, Sheriff. He walked through that campground and he laid his hand on that poor little girl's soul."

"We think it might have been someone more human than that, sir," she explained. "Is there anything you can recall about that night that might help us find the girl's killer?"

Ezekiel frowned. "I spoke about it that night with Paul. He was home from seminary school for a week. I told him that Sheriff Howard was right about closing the campground. No one needed to be there again. I told him we were going to deed the land to the state."

The back door opened and Keith walked in, putting down a few books on the gray-and-chrome counter. "Hi, Sheriff, Deputy."

Ezekiel's face lit up. "Here he is now! Paul, come in and speak to the sheriff about that night when the girl was killed."

FOUR

KEITH SMILED AT them as he took off his jacket. "Sorry, Sheriff. Sometimes, Granddad gets a little confused. Maybe there's something I can help with."

"I wanted to speak with your father again," Sharyn told him. "I met him this morning out at the campground."

Keith shook his head, and then went to help his grandfather pour coffee into four cups. "Did he tell you his whole theory about how evil the place is and how it shouldn't be re-opened?"

"Yes, he did."

"Paul, you were home that night," his grandfather continued.

"I'm Keith, Granddad. Remember?"

Ezekiel looked at his grandson carefully. "Oh, Keith! Of course, it's you! Where's your father?"

"I don't know, sir. He's probably at the church."

"That's right!" Ezekiel looked at Sharyn and Ernie. "He's at the church for a baptism. Maybe he could speak with you later."

"That would be fine, sir." Sharyn gave him her card. "He could give me a call when he's free."

"You want to talk to Dad about his theory on the devil, Sheriff?" Keith wondered skeptically.

"No, we're just talking to people who might recall some details about that night that were overlooked in the records," Ernie told him.

Keith smiled. "Well, I guess I can't help. I was just a baby."

"Is your mother still alive, son?" Ernie wondered.

"No, sir. Kristie didn't tell you?" He smoothed his hand over the cool surface of the kitchen table. "I'm adopted. I never knew my real parents. They brought me here when I was three, when the orphanage closed down."

"Kristie didn't mention it," Sharyn replied.

He shrugged. "They said I was the proverbial doorstep baby. There wasn't even a note. They had no name or anything else that could tell them who I was or where I belonged."

"You were lucky to be taken in like you were, son," Ernie told him.

"I know, sir."

"Didn't Pastor Reynolds ever marry?"

"No, ma'am. He said he was too busy with the church and keeping me out of trouble to find a woman who'd put up with us." Keith laughed. "I think he was just too stubborn for any woman to live with!"

Ezekiel frowned. "You shouldn't talk about your father that way, boy! There's no respect anymore! No one lives by the rules the way they should! Why did Moses bother to find the Ten Commandments?"

"It's okay, Granddad," Keith soothed him. "I'm sorry."

"Have your father give us a call, please, Keith," Sharyn asked. "We have to go. Thanks for the coffee, sir."

"My pleasure, ma'am. You're the sheriff, aren't you?"

"Yes, sir, I am."

Ezekiel frowned. "A woman's place is with her family."

"Yes, sir."

"You should be having a family of your own."

"Yes, sir. Thank you. See you later, Keith."

"Thanks, Sheriff."

They left the old house. Sharyn had the distinct feeling that it was watching them. She shook her head to clear it of that notion. Next thing you know, she'd be thinking the devil *had* killed that little girl!

"Well, maybe your thinking wasn't that far off," Ernie suggested when they were driving down the road back towards Diamond Springs. "The good pastor didn't see fit to tell you that he was home when the murder happened in the campground."

"How can we be sure? I think anything we get from the senior pastor isn't going to be viable. He thought Keith was his son."

"We'll have to check, I guess. Probably has Alzheimer's. That's the way my daddy started."

"Funny how they both mentioned Keith getting into trouble," Sharyn considered. "Let's check it out."

Ernie looked at her. "Do we think he might have crawled over there as a baby and killed that little girl? Or are we checking up on him because he might be a bad choice for Kristie?"

"Actually, I'm the county sheriff and the campground falls into my jurisdiction. I'm thinking about not allowing it to re-open until we know something more about what might have happened there twenty-five years ago. But I also have a right to question any of the staff who might be a problem."

Ernie took out his cell phone. "It's your neck when Kristie finds out you're investigating her boyfriend."

"I know."

He laughed. "I recall that Davis boy you dated a few times your freshman year of college. Your daddy hated him! He swore he was gonna ruin you!"

Sharyn thought about Ron Davis. "Did you investigate him?"

"Down to what his favorite food was for breakfast."

Sharyn smiled. "Well, then you better do background checks on all the counselors who are going to be working at the campground. That way it won't look suspicious. And I don't want any surprises if we open the camp again."

"Whatever you say, Sheriff."

"Ernie!"

"What?"

"Never mind."

Kristie was waiting for her when they reached the office. "I need to see you."

Ernie shrugged and went to his desk.

Knowing there was no way Kristie could have found out about her investigating Keith already, Sharyn smiled at her younger sister. "What's wrong?"

"In your office, please," Kristie replied, marching towards Sharyn's office.

"Hold my calls," Sharyn told Trudy. "Any messages?"

"Nick called. He apologized, but he said he was too sick to come to work. He sounded terrible."

"What about the info on the suitcase?"

"He said he gave it to Keith."

"Keith?"

Trudy looked at her. "That's what he said."

Sharyn frowned as she joined her sister. Why hadn't Keith given her the information when she'd seen him at the house?

"Sharyn, I want to know why you've put off opening the camp," Kristie demanded, before the door was even shut.

Sharyn sat behind her father's big desk and looked at her sister. She looked like her mother when she was angry. Her lips became a thin line and her eyes narrowed. It made Sharyn shudder to think about it.

"Kristie, I didn't put off opening the camp. Yet. I asked the men who were going to gravel the area where we found the suitcase to wait until we had a chance to look for anything else that might be there."

"Anything else like what? I've been working on this project for months! You know that!" She suddenly realized that her sister had used the word *yet*. "Are you saying you might not let us open it?"

"I want to be sure it's safe."

"After one murder, twenty-five years ago?"

"It hasn't been open since then. And there might have been two murders that night. That dress and suitcase didn't belong to the little girl who died in the cabin, Kristie. We don't know who it belonged to yet. I'm not sure if I'm comfortable opening the campground again."

Kristie jumped up from her chair with tears in her eyes. "You could have told me before I put all of this work into it!"

"I didn't know!"

"Do you have some reason to think the murderer might still be out there?"

"I don't know," Sharyn conceded. "That's the problem."

Kristie flung open the door to Sharyn's office. "Dad wouldn't have done this! He would've stood by his word!"

Sharyn shook her head as Kristie stormed out of the building.

"Your daddy wouldn't have talked about opening that campground at all," Ernie told her after Kristie had gone. "He always believed Jacob was right to shut it down." He laid some papers on her desk. "Cari's out for lunch, but here's what she came up with on the counselors at the original camp. There were three teachers from Diamond Springs Elementary school, one of them Selma, and five college students. The counselors each slept in one of the cabins. They didn't know anything was wrong until that morning when the girls started screaming."

"But we have their names?"

"Yep. Cari does a good job. She's already found the other teachers."

"Great. You have lunch with Annie today, don't you?"

"Sure, but you could come along," he invited.

She smiled. "I don't think so. Thanks anyway. You two are cute, but not with lunch."

"Cute?" Ernie demanded as they walked out of her office.

"Your Aunt Selma called, Sheriff."

"What do you mean we're cute?"

"Trudy, tell Ernie how cute he and Annie are."

"Oh, Ernie," the woman complied. "You're like two little love bugs together."

"See?"

"I'm gonna go to lunch," Ernie told them. "We don't look like any such thing!"

Sharyn laughed as she watched Ernie leave the office quickly, knowing that Annie was waiting for him. She turned back to Trudy but the other woman wasn't laughing. Her mouth was trembling as she passed her hand roughly across her eyes. "Trudy?"

"I'm sorry, Sheriff! I get so darned mad at myself when I get this way. I know Ben wouldn't have wanted me to be all weepy and stuff. Sometimes, I just can't help it."

"Oh, Trudy!" Sharyn hugged her tightly. "You were married for thirty years! You wouldn't be human if you didn't get weepy about it. Are you sure you didn't come back too soon? You know we'd hold your job open if I had to make David do it."

Trudy smiled at the idea of David handling the desk and the phone. "I was going crazy at home. I need to work. Just that once in a while, I might cry a little. If that's okay."

"As long as I don't have to give this job to David, I don't care what else you do while you're here. Just tell me if you need to do something different or if you need anything. You know all of us are here for you."

"I know," Trudy replied. The phone rang. "Thanks, Sheriff."

"Thanks for coming back, Trudy." Sharyn wiped a tear from her own eye as she turned away. Ben's death had been so sudden and so tragic. Her own mother hadn't been able to leave her bed for weeks after her father was killed. She could barely attend his funeral.

Sharyn put aside the anger that came up when she thought about Ben's death and the possibility that it might not have been an accident. It wouldn't do any good to question it again. Not yet anyway. Not unless they came up with other information. There hadn't been any way to link it to anyone. It had been ruled an accident by three separate peo-

ple. Even Nick had signed off on it as an acciden-
tal death.

She picked up the phone and called her Aunt
Selma. Sharyn hadn't seen her since her birthday
party a few months back.

"I heard you're investigating that murder at the
old campground again. I have something that you
might want to see, Sharyn," her aunt told her on
the phone. "Maybe you could come out for lunch?"

Sharyn glanced at her watch. "Sure. What's up?"

"I'd rather you come out here, if you don't mind,"
her aunt replied. "Can you come?"

"I'll be there in twenty minutes."

It wasn't like Aunt Selma to be mysterious. She
normally said what was on her mind. Sharyn could
tell something was bothering her at the birthday
party but she hadn't had a chance to talk to her. She
was one of Sharyn's favorite people. Not a small
woman, Selma was tall and big-boned. She had the
square-jawed look that the whole Howard family
possessed. When Sharyn looked at her, she saw
her father again.

Sharyn pulled up to the old homestead about
twenty minutes later. The big two-story house was
squat and old-fashioned, like the parsonage, but
the resemblance ended there. Selma Howard had
been born in that house, along with her brother,
T. Raymond. She had cared for her parents there

until they'd died. Her mother had gone first, then her father, Jacob, died in his bed about ten years later, five years after he'd given up being sheriff of Diamond Springs. Losing T. Raymond had been a blow to Selma, but she'd stayed in the old house, surrounded by sweeping pecan trees.

Selma was an artist and her work was everywhere. Colorful flights of fancy flew in the trees and hid in the branches. Selma loved birds. The house was full of them, inside and out, alive and imaginary. They sang and chattered on the porch and the bushes. She had showed a very young Sharyn how to hold still with birdseed in her hand until a bird came to eat from it. They had spent hours together, caring for the birds and making colorful bird feeders. The *Gazette* always did a story on Selma at least once a year. Tourists came and went from the home of the "bird lady."

Today, Selma was alone except for her constant small companions. She'd set lunch outside to fully appreciate the warmth of the glorious spring day. She hugged her niece as she walked into the old white gazebo. "I thought it might be nice to have lunch out here."

"It's warmed up a lot," Sharyn said, taking off her jacket. The sky was bright blue and the birds were nesting in the trees around them, calling to each other. "I think spring is really here this time."

"I think we're past that last frost," her aunt agreed. "Sit down. Tell me what's happened to bring this whole terrible thing up again."

Sharyn told her about the campground while she ate quiche and pecan pie washed down with tart lemonade. "I don't think the devil killed that little girl. But I think the pastor, Paul Richards, might know something about it."

"You know your granddad worried over that case for weeks. He fretted and fussed so much he couldn't even eat."

"Really? Ernie and I were both surprised when we didn't find any of his notes from the case in the file."

"It was more personal to him than the other cases. It was the case that made him retire from the law. He was up for re-election that year and he decided not to run because he couldn't find that little girl's killer. He took it hard and personal."

Sharyn sipped her lemonade and listened to the birdsong. "I didn't know that." She did some quick mental calculations.

Selma looked at her niece. "Roy Tarnower was sheriff for one term before your father beat him fair and square in the next election. Roy always said that it was fixed. He said that your father and the new district attorney did things that should have been illegal."

Sharyn put down her glass. "Jack Winter?"

Selma nodded. "That old rascal has been around awhile. I heard he's supporting Roy this time around. I saw them on television this morning. A vote for Roy Tarnower is a vote to restore Diamond Springs and Montgomery County back to the way it ought to be. There are a lot of folks that will remember Roy."

Sharyn considered the man who was running for sheriff in a new light. He was in his late fifties, only a few years older than her father would have been that year. He had experience and a grudge against her family. He also had Jack Winter on his side.

"Is that why you're not running for office this time?" Selma wondered. "Do you think you can't win against Roy since he has Jack Winter's backing?"

"No." Sharyn shook her head. "I'm just trying to decide if I want to commit to another four years like the last four. Or worse. I don't know if I really knew what I was letting myself in for when I agreed to run in the first place."

"It's not an easy job," her aunt commiserated. "Especially for a woman. I wasn't sure four years ago if they railroaded you into it just to keep it in the same party. But you've handled yourself so well, Sharyn. I've been so proud of you! I just wanted to be sure you weren't backing down from that polecat! I don't care how it looks to anyone else. *I* needed to know."

Sharyn smiled at her aunt. Selma wore her curly red hair longer than Sharyn. It was streaked with gray, but she was still a handsome woman. "I wouldn't back down from a fight with Jack Winter or Roy Tarnower. I'm just having a tough time fighting with myself over it."

Selma nodded. "You should question it. Don't let them take you for granted, Sharyn."

"Mom thinks I should quit and go back to law school. She says she's afraid every time I walk out the door."

"And I don't blame her," Selma agreed. "I worry about you, too. But I wouldn't try to stop you if you're following your calling, like your father was. He had doubts, too, you know. Just like my father. It's not easy upholding the law. You see terrible things and have to do terrible things. Your granddad killed twenty-two men and one woman in his career as sheriff. He was never proud of it. But he was proud of Diamond Springs."

"I never knew Dad had doubts," Sharyn confessed. "He never told me."

"Every time before an election, he thought it over again. He wouldn't want you to do any less." Selma smiled at her. "You are so like him."

"What about you, Selma? Did you see anything out at the campground?"

Selma handed her three journals. "These belonged to your granddad. As soon as I heard that you might be looking into that old murder, I brought them out. He wrote them while he was looking for the killer at the campground. I thought they might be useful to you."

Sharyn looked at the old, handwritten text with awe. "Thanks. They might be. I'd like to know what he thought about while he was investigating the crime."

"Those books have everything in them that he couldn't put into the public records. I know he'd want you to have them." Selma took a deep breath. "As for me. I didn't know anything about the murder until the next morning, like everyone else."

"Which cabin did you sleep in?"

"Number seven. I could see the fifth cabin from where we were. The teacher who slept there was a friend of mine. Margie Madison. She died from heart failure a few years back. It was a terrible thing, Sharyn. I've never forgotten the children's faces that morning."

"Did you actually see the dead girl?"

"No. I had my hands full keeping my girls from panicking. They herded us onto buses right away and I never went back."

"Was there anything, *anything,* that seemed odd or out of place?" Sharyn asked.

Selma smiled and pushed her hair back from her eyes. "It was a long time ago, Sharyn. But I can't recall anything that seemed out of place. The camp had been open forever and we told the old ghost stories. I don't believe the devil killed that little girl, but the place does have an air to it, doesn't it?"

"It does."

"I'm sorry I couldn't be more help," Selma said. "I have a favor to ask, Sharyn."

Sharyn looked up at her aunt. "Whatever I can do." She knew her aunt hated to ask anyone for help. That she would ask must mean it was serious.

"Look around you, Sharyn. This is Howard land as far as the eye can see. Your great-great-grandfather homesteaded this land. He built a cabin here and was killed by thieves when he was twenty-four. His wife and three sons kept it going. They held on to it through the Civil War. The house was burned but they built this one after the war was over. They planted new crops and they went on with their lives. They handed this land to the next generation. This is your land when I die, Sharyn. Or at least, it was going to be your land."

"What's wrong, Aunt Selma?"

"The Interstate is coming through here, Sharyn. I got the letter two days ago. I spoke with my attorney but there doesn't appear to be anything that can be done. The highway commission is dead set on putting it through here. *Through my home!*"

Sharyn shifted uncomfortably in her chair. "I don't know what I can do, Aunt Selma. I've been to houses where the people have chained themselves to the porch to keep from going and I've had to arrest them. Change is happening in this area. It isn't always nice."

"Nice? Sharyn, this is your family home! There has to be something you can do!"

Selma Howard had never asked for a thing from her niece, even though she had given so much to Sharyn's life. Sharyn knew she couldn't flatly refuse to do anything. "I'll look into it. If your lawyer couldn't find a loophole, though, I may not be able to do anything."

Selma's eyes, so like T. Raymond's, grew hard. "If there's nothing legal to do, Sharyn, then you might as well plan on arresting me! I will not let this place go without a fight! Our family died to keep this land. I don't see how I, or *you,* can do less!"

They were at an uncomfortable impasse. Sharyn left the house soon after. Selma gave her the journals, five jars of vegetable soup she'd canned, a loaf of freshly-baked bread, and a whole pecan pie.

Selma waved to her as she left but Sharyn's heart was heavy with what her aunt expected from her.

She knew this meant everything to Selma, but she balked at using her position as sheriff to save her family's home. Wouldn't that put her on the same level with Jack Winter? She wouldn't have killed anyone, but she had put people in jail and taken them from their property when they wouldn't leave. How could she make an exception in Selma's case?

She still had some time left before she had to go back to the office. She called the morgue but no one had seen Nick. She swung by his apartment and climbed out of the Jeep carrying the bread, some soup, and the pie. She needed to know if he had given those files to Keith. She would just stop by and drop off the food. She would politely ask if Keith had the files, then she would wish him well and leave.

It occurred to her that she had never seen Nick's apartment. She'd driven past it many times, since it was situated on the side of Diamond Lake near the high school. It was an old building, probably built at around the same time as the school. Diamond Mountain was its backdrop behind the smooth reflection of the cold lake.

He had probably lived there since he'd come to Diamond Springs, when her father was still sheriff, she considered, looking at the number on the mailbox beside N. Thomopolis. No security. She just walked up the stairs and stood in front of his door.

She was ready to knock but something stopped her hand short of the sturdy wooden door. What was she going to say to him? Maybe he wouldn't want to see her when he was sick. There was a reason he hadn't come into work.

She stood there with cold feet, a loaf of bread tucked under her arm, trying to decide what to do. She had a strong urge to put down the food and ring the doorbell, then run. It was stupid and childish and she knew she couldn't do it. What if someone saw her? And Nick wouldn't eat food he found on his doorstep.

The problem was solved for her when a tiny woman with a sweet, bird-like face saw her standing there in front of the door. "Hands full, dear? Let me help you!" The woman pounded hard on the door then smiled at her. "Are you a friend of Nick's?"

"I, uh, work with him." Sharyn had the options of either running and hoping Nick wouldn't see her, or standing there and hoping he wouldn't answer the door. The door opened slowly. Her heart started pounding.

"Nick! You look like death warmed over! I found this pretty girl standing here in front of your door and I thought I better knock for her. You don't get too much company. Especially *female* company! Not that I haven't offered to help you out. What's wrong with you anyway? Why aren't you at work?"

Nick was standing in the doorway in a dark robe. He needed a shave and his feet were bare. "Thanks, Mrs. Jalowski."

"No problem. Look, she even has food for you. She can cook! Are you a security guard, dear?"

"No," Nick said in a raspy voice. "She's the sheriff."

"The sheriff? Oh, I know what you mean. I know we have a lady sheriff. Why aren't you running against that other fellow?"

"I'm really sick, Mrs. Jalowski." He coughed a few times to prove it. "I'm probably contagious."

"Oh, dear! I'll see you later then, Nick. Good luck, Sheriff!"

Nick turned away from the door, but turned back when Sharyn made no move to follow. "Are you really a vampire and you can't come in until I invite you?"

"No," Sharyn replied, already too embarrassed to care. "I'm a Southern girl with better manners."

Nick swept his arm wide. "Please, come in." He started coughing again. "Sorry. Everybody had this in New York. I guess I brought it back with me."

Sharyn stepped into the room and closed the door behind her. The room was a mess. She vaguely recalled Nick telling her that when women saw his apartment, they turned and ran the other way. Fortunately, the room was dark so she probably wasn't seeing the worst of it. "I brought you some soup. And bread."

"And pie," he finished for her. "Thanks. You didn't, uh, cook it, did you?"

"No," she denied. "My Aunt Selma sent it."

"Good."

"What?"

He shrugged. "You're the one who told me you couldn't cook!"

"I should go," she said, making room for the food on a cluttered table. "I hope you feel better."

"I'm sorry," he apologized. "I didn't mean to insult your cooking."

She smiled. "You're right. I don't cook. There's nothing to insult."

"Did Keith give you that information?" Nick asked, changing the subject to the more serious matters at hand.

"No. I saw him out at the parsonage, but he didn't mention it."

He shook his head, but was sorry when he did, because it felt like it was going to fall off. "I was hoping he was going to be reliable."

"It was just one time. Maybe he didn't think about it. He was surprised to see us."

"What were you doing out there?" he asked, picking up the jar of soup. "And why won't the top twist off of this jar?"

Sharyn looked at him. He was trying hard to unscrew a sealed jar top. "I'll get it."

In ten minutes, she had him sitting at the tiny table in the kitchen with a napkin and a bowl. She had the soup in the microwave and the bread sliced and buttered. She was telling him about her talk with all three members of the Reynolds' family and her visit to Rebecca Liston's home. He closed his eyes and listened to her, not sure if it was the medication he was taking, or the fact that she was there with him, that gave the whole thing a dreamlike quality.

"Are you all right?" she asked finally when she put the hot soup in front of him.

"Fine." He opened his red-rimmed eyes. "I'm really feeling a lot better. I should be able to work tomorrow."

"I'm glad." She smiled at him. "Do you have any juice?" She looked around and found some in the refrigerator. Surprisingly, the kitchen was spotless. It looked as though it was never used.

"You can tell I eat out a lot," he said, following her eyes. "It sounds like you have two separate murders committed out there at around the same time."

"I was thinking that the dress we found might have belonged to the killer."

"I don't think so," he said, tasting the soup. "This is good. I showed you the cuts in the dress. Those were definitely stab wounds and they were from downward slashes. The killer was taller than the girl in the 'Holly Hobbie' dress. The suitcase was probably beside her when she was attacked. That's how it got arterial spray on it."

"Why put the girl's dress in the suitcase after killing her?"

Nick shrugged. "I don't know. You'll have to ask the killer."

"We haven't found anyone else who was reported missing from the camp. I'm going to check on one of the teachers this afternoon. We're looking for the other counselors."

"What about the other children?"

"They don't remember much. One of them is dead. Another lives in Wyoming. Ed remembers about as much. He was living here at the time."

"What about Ernie?"

"He was away in the Army. My aunt gave me my granddad's journals from the time he was investigating the case. They might be some help. She told me that he wouldn't run for re-election after this case because he couldn't find the killer. I think he might have believed it was the devil, like a lot of other people."

Nick looked at her thoughtfully. "You don't believe that, do you?"

"No. I don't know what to believe yet, but I do

know that it wasn't a ghost or a demon that killed either one of those girls. Whether we can find the person who did it after all this time is another story."

He smiled. "You found Billy Bost's killer. It was a longer time."

"*That* was pure dumb luck!"

"*That* was being a good sheriff!"

She glanced at her watch. "Anyway, I have to get back to work. Could you have some of your students go over the area where we found the suitcase before they pour the gravel?"

"Sure. I can't get out there before tomorrow afternoon. Can you have someone meet us out there?"

"I'll be out there." She studied him with a worried frown. "I hope you're better tomorrow."

"I hope so, too. I'll call Keith." He stood with her, holding his hand on his robe. "Thanks."

"No problem. We wouldn't have eaten all that soup anyway. And pecan pie is next to sloth in my mother's book of sins."

"No, I meant for not running away."

"Oh." She felt her face turn red. "I wasn't *really* going to leave the food and run away. I mean—"

He smiled at her. "I was talking about not running away when you saw the mess in my apartment. What were *you* talking about?"

"Nothing," she replied brightly. "I have to go. Take care of yourself. Call me if you need me."

Nick closed the door after her hasty retreat. *Call me if you need me,* she'd said. He laughed to himself. He didn't think her cell phone could stand the strain!

FIVE

REED HARKER, the head commissioner, called for order in the room. The county commission meeting was going to start on time for a change.

"I hate these things," Ed whispered.

"They go with the job," Ernie whispered. "At least they're not gonna talk to us."

"We have quite a bit on the agenda for today so let's move it along," Harker, a commissioner from one of the new subdivisions outside of town, told the group. "Is Sheriff Howard here?" He looked out into the small crowd that consisted mainly of reporters.

Sharyn stood up. "I'm here, Mr. Harker."

"Good morning, Sheriff. How are you today?" Mrs. Fontana asked pleasantly.

"You can tell they're up for election," Ernie whispered.

"Just fine, ma'am."

"Getting right to the first problem, Sheriff. We have a request from your office for more money for hiring extra deputies, overtime, and a few other things," Harker began.

Sharyn braced herself for a battle. "Yes, sir. If I could explain—"

"Oh, you've done an eloquent job of it here already, Sheriff," the man told her. "We've talked about your request and done some figuring, and with the new tax base, we're prepared to grant your requests."

"You're...just like that?"

"Yes, Sheriff." Harker smiled at her. "We know how important it is to keep this community free from crime and as a good place to raise our children. To this end, we are proposing to add five hundred thousand dollars to the sheriff's department's annual budget."

Reporters wrote quickly while photographers snapped pictures of everyone in the room, especially the commissioners.

Sharyn knew she'd see a surprised look on her face in the paper the next day. "Thank you, sir. This will make a difference in the quality of life in our community."

"Thank you, Sheriff Howard, for bringing it to our attention. We do ask that you come to us with the requests for this extra money to add to the budget as needed. You'll be receiving a copy of this new budget in the mail by the end of the month."

"We have some new business, Sheriff, if we can take some more of your time," Charlie Sommers began from his chair beside the head commissioner. "It's about your request for reinstatement of a separate animal control agency. I'm afraid that just won't fly, Sheriff."

"Mr. Sommers, it's all we can do to keep up with human problems, sir," Sharyn replied. "We just don't have the time or the expertise to deal with cows and dogs."

"Well, at least we have the Department of Wildlife that keeps you from dealing with wild animals, Sheriff. It's not that we are unaware of what you do for this town. I am more aware than most after the tragic death of my daughter. That's why I voted for the extra resources for the sheriff's department. But for now, we're going to have to use that extra money for animal control as well. Surely, with the extra deputies, you should be able to handle the problem."

The cameras and the reporters focused on Charlie Sommers's face when he spoke about his murdered daughter. She was the first homicide in Diamond Springs after Sharyn took office.

Sharyn looked away, not believing that the man was trading on his daughter's murder. It was obvious that they found it cheaper to throw some extra money at the sheriff's department than to create and maintain another animal control unit. They were getting good press about the money. He didn't need to remind people about his daughter, Carrie, who'd been found strangled in the school parking lot.

"And regarding the re-opening of the Bell's Creek campground," Mrs. Fontana said briskly. "The county holds the deed to this property, Sheriff. Unless you have some tangible evidence of danger that would prevent the plan for the children's camp from going through, I suggest we work with the plan we have."

"I have a problem with that, ma'am," Sharyn objected at once.

"Is there something besides a murder twenty-five years ago, Sheriff?" Harker asked. "Because if not, the state has funded part of this project to bring in impoverished children who otherwise wouldn't have access to this type of environment. We've all worked very hard to get this project off the ground."

"We may have evidence of a second crime, sir."

There was a buzz in the audience.

"You mean there's been another murder?" Mrs. Fontana asked, glancing at her fellow commissioners. "Why wasn't I informed?"

"We don't know for certain yet," Sharyn hurried to assure her. "We found possible evidence of another crime that may have occurred around the same time as the first homicide."

"You don't know for *certain?* The crime *may* have occurred? And all this was *twenty-five* years ago?" Harker pressed her. "We need more than that. This camp is the pilot project for a series of camps across the state! Unless you have proof that there's still a murderer running around loose out there, we all feel the camp should open on schedule next week."

"I can't prove anything yet," Sharyn admitted. "But if we re-open the camp and something tragic happens, it'll be too late."

The commissioners talked amongst themselves for a few minutes. Then Harker turned to Sharyn. "Is that all you have, Sheriff?"

"Right now. But I need some extra time to investigate."

"There will be counselors at the camp, along with state aides and plenty of press. This is a real coup for our area. I think it's going to be fine, Sheriff. Let's get moving on it." Harker smiled at her. "I think that's all. Thank you for coming, Sheriff Howard."

"Thanks for listening," Sharyn muttered, walking out of the room.

Ernie and Ed followed her. There were more reporters standing on the courthouse steps with Senator Talbot, Kristie, and Keith. Talbot was already accepting the credit for keeping the state campground program on track.

Kristie and Keith were his shining examples of today's youth leading the way.

Kristie looked up as Sharyn walked out but then looked away quickly. Sharyn knew what had happened. She had been politically outmaneuvered with Kristie's help. Kristie wanted her project to move forward and she had asked Talbot for his help. Sharyn kept going down the stairs.

"Do you think this happened because you're a lame duck, Sheriff?" Foster Odom asked, jumping in her face at the bottom of the stairs.

Sharyn glared at him, then considered how she could use him to her own benefit. "There may have been two murders committed out there, Mr. Odom. One of them we know about. We only have evidence of the second. If anyone knows of another girl who didn't come home from that camp twenty-five years ago, they should get in touch with the sheriff's office right away. Thank you."

Foster Odom grinned at her smugly. "Thank you, Sheriff. I'll print this for you. But I get an exclusive when you decide *if* you're running for sheriff again."

She nodded. "Done." She turned to walk away, but found that Keith and Kristie were at her side.

"Sheriff, I'm sorry. When I saw you I forgot to give you this report we got back from the state lab on the stuff in that suitcase." Keith handed her a red folder.

"Where did ya see Sharyn?" Kristie asked with a suspicious gleam in her blue eyes.

"She was at the parsonage, talking to Granddad. But you wanted to see Dad, didn't you, ma'am?"

Sharyn sighed. "Yes. But thanks for the information. I'll catch up with your dad, Keith."

Keith smiled and turned to leave, but Kristie stayed to glare at her sister.

"I came to tell you that I was sorry about having to talk to the senator," Kristie said. "But you were spying on Keith, weren't you?"

"Kristie—"

"He didn't murder anyone twenty-five years ago! I suppose his only crime was dating the sheriff's sister!"

Sharyn didn't have time to respond before Kristie left her. Keith smiled sheepishly, then followed Kristie to the sidewalk. Sharyn stared after them.

"What now?" Ed asked, pretending he hadn't heard anything that Kristie had said.

"Now we find out what else Cari has been able to dig up about the campground. And we talk to the other counselors."

"And the camp re-opens next week?" Ernie questioned. Sharyn shrugged. "Unless we can give them a better reason *not* to open it."

Ed shook his blond, curly head. "I think I liked

it better when calling a place evil was enough to shut it down!"

Ed, Ernie, and Joe each went out to interview a counselor, since they were at different ends of the county. Sharyn and Cari worked on the computers and answered calls that came after the afternoon *Gazette* printed Sharyn's request for information on missing people from the campground. None of them turned out to be real leads. They were all hearsay and stories about the campground and the Bell's Creek area. Foster Odom called to remind Sharyn that she owed him one for printing her story.

Cari sighed, exhausted, and rubbed her eyes. "I think I'd rather be out on the street catching cows."

"With the extra money from the commission," Sharyn responded, "you'll be able to get your chance."

"You mean you'll be able to make me a full deputy when I finish my training?"

"That's what I mean," Sharyn said, not taking her eyes from the computer screen.

"Will I really have to go after cows?" Cari asked with her nose wrinkled.

"Yes. We're still animal control for Montgomery County. That includes dogs, cats, cows, and the occasional stray horse."

"Why don't they just hire someone to do that job?" Cari demanded.

"They did," Sharyn told her. "They hired *you!*"

"About what David said, Sheriff," Cari began, after thinking about it. "I just want you to know that I didn't ask him to say that. I mean, it's not like we're engaged or anything. We've only gone out on a few dates."

"I understand, Cari. Don't worry about it."

Cari looked up at Sharyn. "Why do you keep him?"

"Excuse me?"

"Well, I've heard rumors. And I was here when he left Beau Richmond alone and he was killed. Everyone thought you should let him go then."

Sharyn stared at her. "Did *you?*"

Cari swallowed hard. "A man was killed. I…I don't know."

"David's a good deputy," Sharyn said. "That's the only way I make my decisions. I don't listen to what other people think I should do."

Cari nodded and looked back at her computer screen. She shivered, glad that the sheriff had looked away. She knew everyone said the sheriff was fair and tolerant, but she had the kind of eyes that could burn a blue hole in your soul. Cari had a hard time looking straight into them. It didn't surprise her to learn that the sheriff wasn't afraid of the devil at Bell's Creek.

At noon, they still had only located one of the

last two college students who had been counselors at the campground. Sharyn rubbed her eyes and sat back from her computer.

"You might as well quit for lunch," she told Cari. "I'm meeting Nick and his students out at the campground. I'll let you come in later and see if you have better luck with the last one."

"Thank you, Sheriff Howard," Cari said very formally. "I appreciate the chance you've given me."

"You're welcome." Sharyn smiled. "It'll be nice to have another woman up here to talk to."

Cari stared at her as she stood up. "Really? I mean, I didn't think you would—"

"Notice whether you were a man or a woman?"

"No. Care. I didn't think you would care."

Sharyn stood up, too. "Between you and me, Trudy has been the only one that's kept me sane working with Ed and Joe and Ernie and David and Nick!"

"Don't you believe it!" Trudy popped her head around the corner of the room. "She's not really sane. No one here is! I'm going to lunch."

"See you later, Trudy."

Cari laughed. "I'm glad I can be here for you, Sheriff."

"I'm glad too, Cari. I'll call in after I go to the campground to see if anything's turned up."

Sharyn drove out to the campground by herself.

Students were already swarming over the would-be parking area like ants on a picnic lunch. They each carried small plastic bags and wore latex gloves.

Nick was seated on a big tree stump, drinking coffee from a Thermos bottle. He was bundled up against the unusual cold and damp. The fog was rising off the open ground. In the distance, the creek was splattering against rocks, full with spring thaw from the mountains. The dam on the river, built forty years ago, had prevented any more flooding of the Bell's Creek area.

"What a wonderful place for a children's camp," he said dourly.

Sharyn hardly glanced at him. "Have they found anything?"

"Probably not," he admitted. "They probably won't find anything. Even before the grader came through, it was all probably lost twenty years ago in the underbrush."

She saw Keith Reynolds with the group of students. "Still thinking about hiring Keith?"

He nodded. "I talked with him this morning. He's going to work part-time until he finishes school next year."

"That's good."

"Coffee?"

"No." She didn't look at him, still focused on the group of students.

"Is something wrong?"

"Nothing unusual." She turned to him. "Would you like to take a look at the cabin?"

He shrugged. There probably wouldn't be any evidence there, but she might be more willing to talk away from the students. "Sure."

They walked together in silence across the damp ground. Fog swirled around their feet and ankles.

"Is that the infamous creek I hear in the distance?" he asked quietly.

Sharyn listened. "Yes."

"Sharyn, you don't have my cold, do you?"

"No, I'm fine."

"You don't sound fine."

Her cell phone rang. "Sheriff Howard."

"We talked with the other teacher, Sheriff," Ernie told her over the phone. "She doesn't even recall being there. Her daughter says she's a mite forgetful. I'm heading back for lunch. How's the search going at the campground?"

"Nothing yet, Ernie."

"Okay. Talk to you later."

"Bye." She closed her cell phone and put it back into her pocket.

"Nothing yet from the survivors? I saw the bit in the paper yesterday about you asking anyone with information to come forward. What did you have to promise Odom to get his help?"

"An interview," she answered. "Here's the cabin."

Nick started to open the front door.

"It doesn't go anywhere," she explained. "You have to go in through the side."

He frowned. "What's the idea of that? I never went to camp as a child. Is that some game?"

"Only here." She told him about the tales of the devil and how the builders of the camp were trying to fool him. "All the cabins are built that way."

"Weird," he remarked, walking into the cabin through the side door.

"It was a camp for poor children," she reminded him. "I suppose they were happy with anything."

"And Rebecca's bed was at the bottom of these stairs?" he asked, looking up at the stairway that led to the ceiling. "That seems easy enough."

"But there's nothing up there. I couldn't see anywhere that looked like an access point. They couldn't find it twenty-five years ago either. The door and windows were closed and bolted shut."

"Did you check on the roof?"

Sharyn gazed up at the ceiling. "No. If the killer couldn't get in this way, what would be the point?"

He shrugged. "I don't know. But doesn't it seem obvious? Six little beds. The one chosen is the one at the base of the stairs that don't seem to go anywhere. The killer got in and out without any of the sleeping girls waking up."

Sharyn watched him walk up the stairs and carefully examine the ceiling. He brought out a magnifying glass and looked at the wood grain but there was no difference. "Maybe it was just to throw us off."

"That's why I didn't go up on the roof," Sharyn explained.

He started back down the stairs and one of the ladder-like rungs cracked under his weight.

"That's another reason I didn't go up there. I was with Kristie when the county told her this place wasn't safe. It's just waiting to be demolished."

"It doesn't make sense, though, does it?" Nick suggested, reaching the floor safely. "Unless the killer was already in the room."

"The counselor who was sleeping here wasn't small enough to have worn that dress we found. She's dead. The other five were children," she reminded him. "Are we suggesting a child killed Rebecca then put her bloodstained clothes into the suitcase?"

Nick shook his head. "That wasn't Rebecca's blood on that dress. Unless there was a knife fight between the two girls."

"But wouldn't that have left some of Rebecca's blood on the other dress?" Sharyn conjectured.

"Professor Thomopolis!" A student almost tripped

coming through the open side door into the cabin. "Come quick! We found something!"

Nick and Sharyn hurried from the cabin, following the girl who ran ahead of them.

"We didn't touch it," another student told them. "I picked it up with the tongs and put it into the plastic bag." The boy's glasses slipped down on his nose while he held out the bag for Nick to inspect.

"It looks like a pocketbook," the girl who came to get him said in awe.

"Duh!" another girl added.

Sharyn knew her from Darva Richmond's murder investigation. "Hello, Megan."

"Hi, Sheriff. Nice gun."

"Thanks." Sharyn glanced at her. "So, you think it looks like a pocketbook, too?"

"Obviously. A little rotted and out of fashion, but that's definitely what it is."

Nick put on his gloves and examined the purse through the plastic bag. "Good work, A-Team. I think it's time to head back to school now and unwrap our gift."

"I need to be excused," Keith said to Nick in a low voice.

"What's wrong, Keith? Did it finally get to you?"

"No." Keith looked around himself at the other inquiring eyes. "I just need to be excused."

"Sure. We'll talk later. I can drop you off with the van."

"That's okay. I can walk from here." Keith nodded to Sharyn. "Sheriff."

"Keith."

"What's up with him?" Sharyn asked Nick when Keith had disappeared between the pine trees.

"I think I know. Look!" He pointed to Ezekiel Reynolds, wandering between the trees. "Keith told me they're having a hard time with his grandfather wandering away. It's one of the reasons he decided to go to school here. The good pastor doesn't want to put his father in a home, if he can help it. But Keith says the old man is as strong as a horse and twice as devious!"

Sharyn watched the argument between grandfather and grandson. "Looks like he might not have a choice." She turned back to Nick. "I'm going back to see what Cari has turned up. Let me know what you find out about the pocketbook."

"Sure. Sharyn?"

"Yes?"

He glanced at her set face. "Never mind. Just be careful, huh? There's something creepy about this place."

"Not you, too!"

Nick shrugged and walked away.

The afternoon dragged by and there was no more

real evidence collected. Ed called in at about three to let them know that he was bringing someone in on assault charges. Sharyn put on her jacket and picked up her backpack. The back door flew open and Ed flew in behind it. There were sounds of scuffling from the parking lot, then Joe was pushing someone in through the open door past Ed.

"We'll have to put you in cuffs if you don't come along quietly," Joe told the assailant.

"Put me in cuffs! Send me through the system! I want the world to know about the injustice that is being done!"

"Aunt Selma?" Sharyn gasped.

"I want to press charges against this woman, Sheriff," a small man with a very large black eye told her as he came in the door after them.

"What happened?" Sharyn demanded.

"She threw a rock and almost put out my eye! All I was doing was surveying for the highway."

"You were on my land!"

"Sheriff?" Ed asked hopefully as he tried to keep the feisty old woman still without hurting her.

"Take her downstairs. Put her in a holding cell," she decided hurriedly. She took off her jacket.

"Sharyn! I'm your only aunt! Jacob Howard's daughter. T. Raymond Howard's sister!"

"You heard the sheriff," Ernie said, following in behind the group. "Take Ms. Howard downstairs."

"Holding only," Sharyn whispered as Ed passed her. "Let me talk to this man."

"Mike Smith," Joe told her as he went along with Ed to try to contain the old woman. "Man, they raise 'em big and strong in your family, Sheriff!"

"I heard that!" Selma Howard yelled. "You can throw me in jail and throw away the key! My name might mean nothing and my family may have forsaken me but I won't let them take my land!"

Mike Smith was nursing his bruised eye. "I want her arrested! I want her tried for attempted murder!"

"Come into the conference room, Mr. Smith," Sharyn invited. "Let's talk about it."

"What's there to talk about?" the man demanded. "Another quarter of an inch and my eye would be gone. She could have killed me!"

"You aren't from around here, are you, sir?" Ernie asked quietly.

"No, but—"

"Ms. Howard is the bird lady around here. Hundreds of people come to visit her every year from across the state. She's an institution."

"She should be *in* an institution!"

"Did you actually see her throw the rock at you, sir?" Sharyn asked, taking out her pen and notebook.

"No, but—" He looked at both of them. "I get

it. You really are related to her, aren't you? So you want me to drop the charges against her."

"There are no charges against her yet, sir," Ernie said.

"We have to take your statement, then go to the D.A. and see if this warrants formal charges."

"Which means you won't do anything? Is that right?"

"That's not right, sir," Sharyn tried to assure him. "But we have to ask you these questions to file a formal document."

"I want someone else," the man replied. "I don't trust you!"

"She's the sheriff of this county, sir," Ernie reminded him.

"I don't care! She's that woman's relative, isn't she? I want someone who'll do something. I want that woman locked up."

Sharyn glanced at Ernie. "This is Deputy Watkins, sir. He's not related to Selma Howard in any way. He'll take your statement."

"Okay." Mike Smith glanced at Sharyn. "Nothing personal, Sheriff."

She nodded. "I'll call and see if a paramedic is available to come and take a look at your eye."

"Thanks."

Sharyn made the call to the paramedics, then

went downstairs to check on her aunt. Selma was by herself in a small cell, sitting on a cot. Her shoes were gone and her hair was in wild disarray. Her dress was torn and dirty. Sharyn sighed, not even wanting to imagine what her father would have said if he were there.

"Aunt Selma?" She opened the cell door.

"Sharyn? What do *you* want?"

"I want to help you. An apology from you would make it a lot easier to convince this man not to press charges against you."

"I will not apologize," Selma said stubbornly. "And I want to be charged. I want my day in court. Maybe all those others you told me about went quietly but I won't just fade away. I won't let them take my home, Sharyn."

Selma was immovable. So was Mike Smith. Sharyn had no choice but to send the paperwork to the D.A.'s office. It took Lennie Albert five minutes to call her back.

"The D.A. wants to see you, Sheriff," Lennie told her.

"I don't want to see him, Lennie," she told her former deputy. "I'm tired of this game."

"There's no night court tonight, Sheriff. If your aunt doesn't get arraigned or the charges aren't modified, she's going to spend the night in jail."

"Tell him to do what he has to do," Sharyn replied, then hung up the phone.

"Sheriff?" Ernie asked.

"I'll make her as comfortable as I can," she said, rubbing her eyes with her hands. "She won't give and neither will he. She's going to have to spend the night here. You and I both know there's nothing I can do to change that at this point."

"Let me call someone," Ernie said.

"Who?"

"Jill Madison-Farmer. I know you don't like her but she's good lawyer."

"Okay." She nodded. "I'm going to spend the night here with Aunt Selma."

"I'll see you in the morning."

"Thanks, Ernie."

Sharyn saw to it that her aunt had an extra blanket and pillow. She took the little heater from her office and put it in the cell. She cleaned the toilet before she hung a blue blanket around the space for privacy.

"All of those things are a direct violation of the safety code for prisoners," a guard told her.

"I'll be upstairs all night. Call me if there's a problem," Sharyn told the man.

"Yes, ma'am."

Selma gazed at her niece through the cell bars.

"This is your fight, too, Sharyn Howard. You can't walk away from it."

Sharyn shook her head. "Good night, Aunt Selma."

SHARYN SAT IN THE CHAIR in her office. She couldn't bear to look at her aunt behind those bars, but she couldn't do anything more to make it better for her. With any luck, Jill Madison-Farmer would be able to represent her and Selma would be free in the morning. The phone rang and Sharyn answered it.

"Please don't tell me that you really have your Aunt Selma locked up for the night!" her mother wailed on the other end.

"Good night, Mom."

"Sharyn—"

Sharyn hung up the phone, then wrapped her coat around her arms. She picked up her grandfather's journal and found her place: *No one saw anything. No one heard anything. Yet a little girl is dead. No task I have ever done has been as terrible as telling her parents that we failed to protect their daughter.*

J.P. and David glanced at Sharyn a few times as they walked by the office during the long night. They didn't ask, and she ignored them. She didn't want to talk about arresting her own aunt. At that moment, she didn't want to think about being sheriff. She couldn't even help one of the people she cared for most in the world.

In the morning, A.D.A. Toby Fisher was at her door. Sharyn had changed uniforms and showered. She'd helped Selma do the same, watching her aunt as she brushed her long hair. Selma refused to speak to her. Sharyn wasn't surprised. Ernie brought in donuts and Selma's lost shoes. Jill Madison-Farmer was there with him. She closeted herself with her client while the A.D.A. tapped his foot impatiently by the coffee maker.

"One of the guards downstairs complained about Ms. Howard receiving preferential treatment," he said to Sharyn. "I'll have to report it."

"Do that." Sharyn turned on her heel and walked away.

"You're taking quite a chance with your reputation," he continued.

"Ever take a look at the size of that gun the sheriff carries?" Ed asked the man with a smooth smile.

The A.D.A. faltered. "She's the sheriff?"

"Yes, sir." Ed replied. "That about sums it up."

"When was the last time she shot someone with that gun of hers?" Joe asked Ed.

Ed considered the question. "I think it was that man who tried to hurt Ernie. Yes, sir. Sheriff's mighty peculiar about protecting her family."

"What are you two talking about?" A.D.A. Fisher asked abruptly. "Are you threatening me?"

"Of course not," Ed assured the man, giving him a small pat on the back. "The sheriff doesn't like lawyers, but she hardly ever shoots one."

"That's enough," Ernie broke up the group at the coffee pot. "Ed, I think you have patrol again. Joe, we're going out to try to talk to that teacher again today."

Joe lifted his chin towards Sharyn's retreating form. "Where's the sheriff going?"

Ernie winked at him. "You know how she doesn't like to fire her weapon until it's been cleaned?"

"Yeah?"

"She's going to have it cleaned."

Toby Fisher left them abruptly, muttering about waiting for the arraignment at the courthouse. Kristie and Faye Howard rushed in from the street, demanding to see both Sharyn and Selma.

"You just missed Sharyn, Faye," Ernie told her. "Selma is in there with her lawyer."

"Sharyn didn't stay with her?"

"That wouldn't be ethical, Mom," Kristie filled in. "She's the sheriff."

"What good is it to be the sheriff if you can't prevent something like this from happening? Your father would've known what to do."

Ernie excused himself, shaking his head. He was glad that Sharyn had gone. She didn't need that grief.

SIX

"I've located two more of the college counselors," Cari said to Sharyn as she walked through the back door to the office.

Sharyn had gone home to shower and change clothes. Reporters were at the gate to the impound lot, but they kept their distance. Foster Odom shouted questions to her as she got out of her Jeep. She ignored him and went quickly into the office.

Ernie was waiting for her in her office. "Ms. Madison-Farmer got your aunt out on bail," he told her. "Your mama took her home. She's scheduled to appear in court next week."

"Good." Sharyn sighed. "At least she won't be here again tonight. I don't think I could take seeing her behind those bars again."

"She couldn't get the charges dropped on her. The D.A. is out to get her."

"That doesn't surprise me either. What about that teacher?"

"No one remembers anything peculiar. Rebecca was a sweet twelve-year-old with no enemies.

They didn't know anything was going on until the screams in the morning."

Sharyn nodded. "Let's take this in the conference room and see what Cari has to say. Is Joe back yet?"

"Not yet. He was having tea with the other teacher." Ernie looked at her closely. "You don't look so good."

"Thanks. I didn't sleep last night. This investigation is going nowhere and my aunt thinks I've abandoned her. I wish my father was sheriff right now."

Ernie glanced up at the picture of her father on the wall. "Your father loved the law. Not lawyers, but the law. He believed in the system. He would have let it work, even if it had been *you* behind those bars."

Sharyn stared at him. "Are you saying he never used his influence?"

"No. I'm not saying anything of the kind. I know he worked a few side deals where he could, and for good reason. But something like this, your father wouldn't have wanted the whole county to question his judgment because of the way he treated a family member."

"I can only do what I think is right," she added. "I don't know how else to live or work this job."

"Your mama is gonna use this as another reason for you to quit," he said.

"I know." She picked up her folder. "Let's go."

They joined the two others in the conference room. Joe had just come back from tea with Ms. Markham.

"I feel bloated," he told them. "I drank five cups of tea before that lady finally came to the point."

"Did she recall anything any different?" Sharyn asked.

"Not a thing. It's like they all wrote the details down together to remember."

"Or worse," Sharyn said, looking through her notes. "Like they all remember the same thing from the paper the way Ed does."

"I could only find two of the counselors that were from local areas. One of them graduated from Diamond Springs High School. The other came from Indian Creek on the other side of the mountains. The other two we found yesterday were from Duke and State. I spoke with the counselor from Duke this morning. She couldn't think of anything she could add to what we already know. But the counselor from State recalled that there were footprints in the ground outside the cabin that morning."

"What kind of footprints?" Ernie asked, sitting forward in his chair.

"Cloven ones," Cari said, wincing. "The two local counselors moved away and I haven't been able to find them yet. The fifth counselor was a woman named Betsy Peterson who had dropped out of college. They have no records for her after that."

"She dropped out after the murder?" Ed asked.

"No, before. I'll keep trying those other two numbers."

"Wait a minute," Sharyn said quickly. "Betsy Peterson?"

"Yes." Cari looked at Joe and Ernie for help.

"EJP. The initials on the locket in the suitcase. Betsy is short for Elizabeth. See what you else you can find out about her, Cari."

"There wasn't anything, Sheriff." The other woman shrugged. "She signed on as a counselor but dropped out of school before the murder. I'm not even sure if she was there."

"Find out," Sharyn told her. "Ernie, get on the phone with the counselors you've talked to. Find out if they remember this Betsy Peterson. You, too, Joe."

"Sheriff! I can't drink any more tea!"

"Do it on the phone then, Joe. Ernie, call the Listons and see if they remember a girl by that name at the camp. And I hate to ask, but could you call my aunt Selma?"

Ernie nodded. "You think Rebecca might have known Betsy Peterson?"

"I think we finally have a place to start. I'm going back out to the campground to meet John

Schmidt. He's going to take a look at the cabin where the girl was killed. I'm hoping he might be able to shore it up so we can get in there safely and take a look around."

"You know they must have investigated all that when old Jacob was out there," Joe said.

"Line two, Sheriff," Trudy said, popping her head around the door. "I think this might be a person who actually knows something about the old campground."

"Thanks, Trudy." She turned back to her deputies. "Forensics is better now. And they were so convinced that the place was evil, even my grandfather. The room was full of six beds and the girls' stuff. It would have been easy to overlook something. Let's get moving! We only have a few days to keep this campground closed down. Despite the senator and the commission, I mean to do just that. Let me know if any of you hear anything that might lead us to Betsy Peterson."

Sharyn left them there and went to take her phone call.

"She's awfully stubborn," Cari said, gathering her folders together.

Joe picked one up for her when it fell on the floor. "She has to be."

"But I don't know if I can find anything else about that woman. It's been a long time."

"Let me get you started," Ernie volunteered. "Once you get the hang of it, you'll be able to find anything."

"And it beats chasing cows in Harmony," Joe quipped.

Sharyn spoke briefly with the woman on the phone before she left the office.

"My great-granddaddy helped build those cabins out there, Sheriff. I'd be glad to send you his original drawings of the campground, if that might help you," the woman said.

"That might help, ma'am," Sharyn agreed.

"I'll just have my grandson run those over to you then. I was wondering if there was anything you could do about my neighbor's dog barking? He lets it bark all night long."

"You can file a complaint, if you like," Sharyn replied. "And I'll send a deputy to talk to your neighbor."

"He wouldn't arrest him, would he? He's a good man. He just has an annoying dog."

"No, ma'am. We don't arrest people with barking dogs. Thanks for calling."

Ernie was helping Cari with the computer search when Sharyn finally signed out of the office. Joe had been called out to help with a drunk and disorderly who had pulled a gun on Ed, then run into the woods. There was another call about a woman in a Mercedes who had shot out a motel window on the Interstate.

Spring fever, Sharyn thought, pulling out of the impound lot. Everyone was going crazy. Her father always said it was the change in the weather and not enough people drinking sassafras like they should. He was a big believer in getting the poisons out of the body. T. Raymond had never touched a drop of alcohol in his life. He claimed it messed up the liver and went straight to the heart.

She smiled. Her father had always claimed he was going to live to be a hundred and die in his daddy's bed. He might have been afraid at times, but he never let on to Sharyn. Aunt Selma said he had his doubts about being sheriff, but he never acted like he had a doubt in his whole life.

John Schmidt called Sharyn on her cell phone before she reached the campground to tell her that he was running late. She had already called Nick. He was leaving the hospital to meet her there. Sharyn got out of the Jeep and walked back to cabin number five. The side door was open but there was no sign of anyone else having been there. She walked inside cautiously and looked around the room. Everything looked the same.

She went back outside and studied the front door that opened into the wall. There was something odd about it. When she pushed against the wall where the door opened, she heard something groan inside the cabin. She went back inside and pushed at the wall again, definitely feeling something give way.

A shadow passed by on the ceiling and Sharyn felt a prickle of fear at the base of her neck. There was a loud groan from the roof timbers but before she could move, the entire ceiling came crashing down on her. She put up her arms to ward off the worst of the weight from hitting her head, but there was too much material. The supporting timber knocked her to the floor and buried her beneath the rubble of wood and shingles. Sunlight danced on the dust motes as the wood settled, and then was still.

NICK PULLED HIS CAR beside Sharyn's Jeep. The creek was crashing against its banks in the distance. He had noticed the first time he'd been there that there were no birds calling from the trees. Even from his apartment in Diamond Springs, he could hear the sound of new frogs getting ready for warmer days. Not at Bell's Creek. He shivered at the random thoughts that went through his head about the place being haunted and cursed. He didn't believe in anything he couldn't see and touch, but he believed that something was wrong about that end of the county.

He didn't see the carpenter's truck that was supposed to be meeting them there but he knew that wouldn't stop Sharyn from going to the cabin to take another look around. The woman was dedicated to the extreme. Nothing stopped her and nothing got in her way. Sometimes, he thought she was as invincible as she seemed. But he'd done the autopsy on her father. No one was invincible.

He walked to the cabin, the ground squelching under his feet. He pushed at the door on the side of the building but it wouldn't open. Frowning, he walked around to the real window and looked inside. The ceiling was gone. The room looked as though it had been through an earthquake. There was no sign of the stairs or…Sharyn! A deep, stabbing fear told him that she was under that pile of wood, metal, and shingles.

"Hey, Nick," John Schmidt hailed him cheerfully as he came around a corner. "Where's the sheriff?"

"I think she's buried under that rubble," Nick told him, ripping off his coat. He used it to shield his hand as he broke through the large glass windowpane. "Call 911. We have to find her!"

"Wait, Nick! It's not safe to go in!"

"Call!" Nick demanded as he pushed himself through the aperture. "The phone's in my car!"

Nick climbed carefully into the room. He looked up where the ceiling had been. There was still some framework but it was mostly gone. Sunlight poured in on the devastating scene in the cabin. Where should he walk? Where had she been when it had fallen on her? "Sharyn? Sharyn, can you hear me?"

He walked carefully around the outer edges of the room. His feet slipped through holes between the timber and broken plywood on the floor.

"I called," John yelled from the window. "Are you sure she's in there?"

"Yes! We have to get this stuff out of here!"

"Let me saw open the doorway and we can start throwing it out," John said. "If she's in there—" He didn't finish the thought.

"Sharyn?" Nick called her name again. "Sharyn, come on! Make some sound! We have to know where you are!" There was nothing but silence. He heard the sound of the saw as John cut through the closed doorway. There was too much scrap against the real doorway to open it. Large, jagged pieces of broken wood stabbing up through the rubble made him feel cold to the point of numbness. He made himself begin to move the wood and shingles towards the wall, one hand at a time.

"Hold on," he told her. "Hold on."

Nick and John worked together in silence, moving the pile of debris out of the cabin. Ernie joined them with Ed and Joe a few moments before the paramedics showed up.

"Nick?" Ernie asked, catching his attention. "Are you sure she's in there?"

Nick nodded mutely. "The stairs are gone but they were in the center of the room. We were looking at them yesterday. She was probably there with them."

Ernie looked at the room and shuddered. He couldn't seem to move.

"Let's cut another hole in that back wall and meet them towards the middle," Joe suggested. "We can get to her faster that way."

"Have them get a stretcher and some oxygen down here," Nick said calmly, belying the sick doubt that twisted inside of him. "She'll need it when we get her out."

Ernie stood completely still.

"Ernie?" Ed put his hand on his arm. "Let's get the saw like Joe said and go from the other side."

"I can't believe—" Ernie rubbed his hand roughly over his face. "Let's do it!"

Sharyn woke up with the sound of the saw ringing in her ears. At first, she thought it was right on top of her. Then she realized what had happened. She was trapped beneath the collapsed roof. She remembered the shadow she'd seen pass over the roof. Someone had set this up purposely. Someone didn't want them to be able to investigate the cabin again. That meant two things: the killer was still alive and still near the campground. And he was willing to kill again.

She tried to speak but dust was caught in her throat. Her head hurt and there was a tight pain around her right knee. Pain was good, she told herself. If she could still feel the leg, it wasn't too bad. They were working to get her out. Nick or John must have realized that she was beneath the debris.

She cleared her throat and tried to yell again. The saw started up just as she yelled, so she knew there was no way they could hear her over it. She waited, trying to be patient and keep from panicking. Something was pressing down on her chest, making it difficult to breathe. She couldn't see anything from beneath the wood. There was insulation in her face but she couldn't move it. Her arms were trapped beneath her. She tried to move them, but it was impossible.

The saw was quiet again. She waited, took a deep breath then yelled as loud as she could.

"What was that?" a paramedic asked. "Did you hear something?"

Everyone stopped moving and waited. In the ensuing silence, Nick thought he could hear his own heart frantically beating.

Sharyn frowned, annoyed that they hadn't heard her. She took another deep breath and yelled again.

"Sharyn!" She heard Nick yell back. "Make some more noise so we can find you!"

"I'm under the wood and stuff," she yelled,

coughing when she got more dust into her throat and lungs. "I'm towards the fake doorway. Or at least I was."

Ernie was there first. He moved a pile of shingles and saw her face. She was scratched up and a little bloody but she was alive. "You almost scared me to death! What were you doing?"

"Being the sheriff," she told him, smiling at him though it pained her to do it. "What they pay me to do."

"They don't pay you to get killed," Nick told her briefly, so glad to hear her voice that he almost wept. "Can you feel your arms and legs?"

"Yes. They hurt," she answered.

"That's good."

"Thanks."

"How's your head? Are you seeing clearly?"

"You look pretty good," she admitted with a grin.

Nick smiled back at her. "I bet you say that to all the men who rescue you."

"Don't try to move yourself," Ernie advised her. "Just let us get you out and the paramedics will take it from there."

"Ernie—"

"There must be some clause in the sheriff's manual about the head deputy taking over if the sheriff is hurt," he told her.

"I remember reading that clause," Ed confirmed.

"If the sheriff gets buried under a house, the lead deputy gets to tell her what to do."

"Only because she's too stubborn to do it otherwise," Joe agreed.

"The county forbids sheriffs or deputies from returning to duty after an accident until there has been a thorough investigation," Nick quoted from the regulations. "That takes the stubbornness right out of you, doesn't it?"

"I'm still wearing my gun," she replied, feeling very tired and cold suddenly. Her teeth began to chatter.

"Cold?" Nick asked.

"Y-yes."

"Shock," Ernie said quietly. "We don't know what's going on yet under those pieces of wood."

"I can see her leg," Joe announced.

"Let's get her out of here, boys," Ed said. "Makes the county look bad to have its sheriff buried alive."

It took another hour to clear enough debris to get her safely out. It was getting dark inside the cabin. Nick had wrapped his suit coat around Sharyn's shoulders. She was still freezing. Ernie was talking to her and holding her hand, keeping her awake when she began to nod off. The paramedics levered the stretcher into the room and they carefully lifted her onto it. They passed her quickly outside through the chain of men who were gathered in the room.

"Let me through! Let me through! I'm her sister!" Kristie yelled as she saw what was happening. She left Keith standing at the new doorway and followed the paramedics to the ambulance with Sharyn.

Nick picked up his jacket where they had dropped it while moving her. He had enough knowledge to help her, but he knew they wouldn't let him, and they would be right. His hands were shaking, cut and bloodied from moving the wood and shingles. He watched Kristie follow the stretcher to the ambulance. All he could do was wait.

"Let's go and have some coffee," Ernie said, heartily slapping his back.

"There's a coffee shop at the hospital," Ed said.

"With the world's worst coffee," Joe reminded them.

"The hospital it is then," Ernie replied cheerfully. "Remember two years ago when that old lady shot you and you thought you might lose your pretty face, Ed?"

"I remember," Ed answered. "How about last year when that crazy guy came after you?"

"Yeah." He looked at Nick. "Ever been shot, Nick?"

"No."

"Well, I think all of us have at one time or another. We'll talk about it over some coffee."

"I think I need something stronger," Nick remarked.

"You must never have had the hospital coffee if you think that," Joe assured him. "Nothing stronger than that!"

"Turpentine!" Ernie quipped. "I rode out with the twins here, Nick. How about a ride back into town?"

"What about Sharyn's Jeep?" Nick wondered.

"We'll pick it up tomorrow. It'll be all right until then."

It was a long night. What with tests and examinations and finding a room, it was 3:00 a.m. before Sharyn was finally settled into a bed. Her head hurt, but they had assured her it was only a mild concussion. Her knee had a few stitches and she had a few bruised ribs. The doctor told her it was a miracle that it was nothing more. Sharyn told them it was just that she had a hard head.

Pleasantly drowsy with medication, she looked out her window at the night sky. She already knew her mother and Kristie were outside the door. Senator Talbot was with them, of course. She realized that his presence at family gatherings of any kind was something she was going to have to expect. Whether she liked it or not, he was going to be a member of their family.

Ernie, Ed, and Joe came in together a short time later. They stood beside the bed, uncharacteristically quiet, looking at her.

She reviewed her troops with a jaundiced eye. "I can't believe all of you are still awake."

"We weren't," Ed admitted with a grin. "We were asleep downstairs until they came and told us we could see you for a minute."

"Thanks for waiting," she said. "And thanks for getting me out of there."

"Did you see anything or anyone?" Joe asked in a practical way.

"Yes and no."

"I'd expect a better answer from you," Ernie added.

"Well, I saw a shadow run across the ceiling, probably the roof. Then it all came down on me."

"So it could've been the devil or it could've been Nick having a bad day?" Ed questioned.

Sharyn laughed, stopping herself when it hurt her ribs. "Something like that."

A nurse came in and told them it was time to leave.

"Where is Nick?" she asked quietly.

"We called him. He's down in the basement working on that pocketbook you found," Joe told her.

"Yeah, he couldn't stand the pressure," Ed answered.

"He was the one who knew you were in that

mess," Ernie told her. "He was working like a demon trying to get you out when we got there."

"Story time tomorrow, gentlemen," the nurse said again. "The sheriff needs her rest."

The three deputies said good-night. Ernie kissed Sharyn's forehead and put his hand on her cheek. "Don't let me come in here tomorrow and find out you left already! You get some rest and take it easy. Okay?"

"Okay." She smiled at him. "Thanks, Ernie."

Sharyn wasn't ready for her mother and Kristie. They were huddled together, wiping away tears. Selma was with them but she stood apart from them.

"I wish you could quit this job tomorrow," her mother said. "This isn't right for a woman to do."

"Hush!" Selma said to Faye. "It's her calling. You can't take that away from her."

"How can you say that?" Faye demanded. "We lost T. Raymond to this job. She put you in jail—"

"She was doing her job," Selma told her in her usual, no-nonsense way. "She serves the whole county and all the people. She can't involve herself in petty arguments, even my petty arguments." She took Sharyn's hand. "I hope you can forgive me for being such a fool."

"You were standing up for what you believe in."

"Well, I won't give up but I know now that I need another plan."

"Well, so does your niece!" Sharyn's mother declared.

"Mom," Kristie said, trying to ease the battle, "I've been stupid and selfish, too. We all have. I wanted to get my way about the campground so I went to Caison for help to go around what Sharyn said. Selma thought she should get special treatment. And you just won't let go of the idea that Sharyn is happy doing this work! And she's good at it!"

"I can see that, Kristie," her mother remarked. "Look at her, all broken up and hurt!"

"Mom," Sharyn argued. "I'm not broken up. Just a little bruised."

Her mother looked at her, then left the room.

"I suppose we should go, too," Selma said with a sigh. "Get better before you go out to battle evil again, please."

"I will," Sharyn said. "Aunt Selma? I think I might have a plan to save the house. It came to me while I was having my head examined."

"Shh." Selma kissed her niece's forehead. "We'll talk tomorrow. Don't worry about anything except getting better."

Kristie bent down and kissed her. "I love you. Get better. I'm sorry about the campground. Maybe you were right."

Sharyn looked out at the night sky again. She

felt sleepy, but she couldn't put her thoughts at ease enough to actually sleep. She wasn't in pain, though, so she didn't call for the nurse. She looked up when Nick came into the room.

"Not sleeping?" he asked.

"No. I'm kind of worried that the ceiling might fall in on me here, and there's so much more to fall," she quipped.

"It wouldn't surprise me," he said. "They're going to take a look at the cabin in the morning and see if it fell down on its own."

"It would give me a good reason to shut the whole place down if it didn't," she replied. "I know the state said it was ready to fall when it was checked out for structural defects a few weeks ago. It just didn't look that bad when we were there. And I think it happened too fast for it to be natural."

"Did you see anyone or anything?"

She sighed. "Only a shadow. Nothing substantial. But we both know it had to be the killer. He has to be protecting himself."

Nick nodded. "I agree. But I don't think it's something you should be thinking about right now."

"Do you have any answers from the pocketbook yet?"

"Yes, but I'm not discussing them with you until you can sit up at your own desk tomorrow or the next day."

"Nick—"

"There's no way you can make me feel any different, Sharyn," he told her. "I had to help dig you out of that scrap heap. I'm not treating you like the sheriff until some other doctor says you're healthy again."

"Like you've ever treated me like the sheriff!"

"What?"

"You heard me. You always treat me like a kid sister who you know is going to make a mistake and you're waiting to tell mom and dad." She looked at him in the dim light, wondering if it was the drugs or the other frustrations in her life that made her talk to him that way.

His eyes were black and deep as he looked down at her. Without another word, he leaned close and pressed his mouth to hers. It was only a brief touch. He stayed close, looking into her eyes. His voice was slightly hoarse when he spoke. "Never a kid sister, Sharyn. Not in this lifetime. Get some rest."

He was gone before she could speak or react in some way. She was glad because she didn't know what she would've said or how she would've reacted. She wasn't herself. She realized that she was holding her fingers to her tingling lips. He *had* kissed her.

It wasn't that she hadn't been kissed by him before. And not that it had been anything more than just a peck on the cheek, as her daddy used to say. Only it wasn't on her cheek. It was full on the mouth. And it was the way he looked at her afterwards and the sound of his voice. *Never a kid sister, Sharyn.*

"Dr. Thomopolis said you were having some trouble sleeping," the nurse said when she bustled in a few minutes later. "Dr. Strickland said that wasn't good." She added something to Sharyn's IV. "Get some sleep, Sheriff. All the bad guys will still be out there to catch tomorrow."

Sharyn smiled as she fell asleep. And it wasn't demons or ghosts or bad guys who filled her dreams.

WITH HER DOCTOR'S best wishes, Sharyn was back on the job the next afternoon.

"I'm fine," she assured everyone who gave her a worried frown. She was limping a little on her hurt knee, but her head felt clear. Her ribs were still sore, but she was ready to get back to work.

She looked at the group of people in the conference room. Ed was doodling hearts and flowers, as always. Joe was playing with his new Swiss Army knife. Ernie was jotting down last-minute notes. Cari dropped most of her papers as she came into the room. Ed leaned to pick them up, and Cari smiled at him.

David walked into the conference room at that moment. He frowned as he watched Ed hand back Cari's papers. "Sheriff." He nodded. "Good to see you back on your feet so soon."

"Thanks, David."

"About that other matter we discussed—"

"Not today, David," Sharyn cut him off.

"Sheriff!"

"Not today, David. Go home and get some sleep. We might need you to work a double shift if we're going to investigate a murder."

"Great," he muttered. "That's what this town needs—another murder investigation!"

"We don't need one," Nick said, coming into the room behind him, "but it looks like we've got one just the same." He took off his coat and laid out thick file folders for everyone in the room. "Or should I say two?"

SEVEN

"HERE'S WHAT WE HAVE, ladies and gentlemen," Nick continued. "What we found was a purse. It contained a hairbrush with a few hundred strands of hair in it. The strands of hair matched the strands we found caught in the ring that was in the suitcase. The blood splatters on the jewelry in the suitcase matched the blood on the suitcase, the dress, and the purse. There was no ID in the purse. But there was this note."

He handed the note in the plastic bag to Sharyn. It was almost completely intact. She read it aloud. "'I'm coming for you tonight. We can start a new life. Don't be afraid. Everything will work out. I love you.'"

"Thanks to the miracle of plastic, the note was in good shape. We know what kind of ink it was written with. We know that the writer was probably a man, left-handed from the incline of the letters. I let a friend of mine whose specialty is handwriting analysis look at it."

"What did we find out about Betsy Peterson?" Sharyn asked Cari.

Cari smiled at Ernie then looked at the papers before her. "I made copies of everything I could find," she said, handing them out. "Elizabeth Peterson was enrolled at the city college for a year prior to the murder. She was a good student, active in extra-curricular activities. She signed up to volunteer as a counselor at the campground, then she dropped out of school two months before the murder. She graduated from Indian Creek High School, with honors, where I found this photo of her."

"Blond," Ernie said, looking at the photo.

"Good-looking," Ed added.

"Where is she now?" Nick asked impatiently.

"That's the thing. No one seems to know. Her parents are dead. Her mother died before she went into college, but her father was still alive until three years ago. I couldn't seem to locate any other relatives," Cari explained.

"Check the emergency numbers on her college application?" Joe asked.

Cari opened her eyes wide, then looked at the application. "She lists her father and an aunt in Indian Creek. I could check on the aunt." Cari beamed at him. "Thanks, Joe."

"No problem. That's why we're a team."

"John Schmidt called in this morning," Ernie

added. "The roof on that old cabin was in sorry shape. But he's pretty sure somebody also sawed off the timbers at the edges of the roof. That shadow you saw on the roof yesterday, Sheriff, was probably someone pushing down hard enough to make the cut beams fall on you. It probably wasn't an accident from rotting timber."

The room was quiet. Sharyn drew a deep breath. "But he can't tell for sure?"

Ernie shrugged. "Not yet. He's calling in another opinion, but the place is a wreck. It could be a few days before he knows for sure."

"I guess that will have to be enough to go to the commission again and request the camp not be re-opened until we finish the investigation," Sharyn concluded.

"I don't know," Ed said. "They're mighty keen on opening it."

"We'll see," Sharyn replied. "In the meantime, Ed is in court today. Joe has patrol. Ernie, you said the teachers don't recall if Betsy Peterson was at the camp?"

"No. They think she might have been but they just aren't sure. And the Listons don't recall hearing the name before."

"Maybe you could check with the two counselors Cari was able to get in touch with. See if they can place Betsy there. Cari, you see what else you can find out about Betsy. She was bound to have friends. And let's see if the aunt is still alive."

"What are *you* doing?" Nick asked her.

Sharyn glanced at him. "I'm going to see the commission members about keeping the camp closed. If there's some other information by then, I'm going to follow up on that. Then—"

"Then that should be it and you should go home," he said briskly.

Sharyn glared at him. "When I'm finished."

"He's right, you know, Sheriff," Ed ventured into the debate.

"And you probably shouldn't drive today," Ernie added.

"Thanks for all your concern, but I'm okay. The doctor said so."

"And he said you should work twelve full hours and drive all over creation?" Nick questioned. A black brow lifted her way. "I don't think so. If he did, I want his license revoked."

"I'm the only one who can talk to the commissioners," she explained.

"Good," Ernie decided. "You stay here and call the commissioners, then you can make any other calls you have to make. If there's any running to do, I'll do it."

Sharyn's knee was throbbing and her ribs hurt.

She looked at all their anxious faces and smiled. "Fine. I'm grounded. Is everyone happy?"

"I think so," Nick said quietly. "I have a class to teach. If you need me, you know how to reach me."

Sharyn watched him walk out of the room. She had dreaded going to the office that morning. She didn't know how Nick would act or if it would be awkward between them. Instead, he was just as quick and sharp as ever. There were no furtive looks. He didn't ask if he could see her in private to talk about what happened between them. In fact, it might not have happened at all.

Bowing to her deputies' wishes and the dictates of her own personal limits, Sharyn called the three commissioners. Mrs. Fontana was sympathetic but uncertain. Senator Talbot was pushing the project. Since the state was involved and clearly wanted to open the camp on time, she was uneasy about trying to stop them.

Reed Harker was very clear on the subject. The state had promised them money for a new playground facility outside the city, close to his home. He wasn't going to upset the plans for shadows and myth.

Charlie Sommers was sympathetic, but felt the cabin wasn't sound in the first place.

"All the more reason not to open the campground," Sharyn argued, frustrated.

"But we know the rest of the cabins are okay," he replied. "They were tested."

"They were tested," she agreed. "But someone is still out there, Mr. Sommers. The camp isn't safe."

"Yes, but you admitted yourself that you and Nick Thomopolis were out there poking and prodding. You shouldn't have been there. You weakened the ceiling, and that's why it fell. No mystery to be solved there, Sheriff. The state is ready to proceed next week. I don't see any reason why we shouldn't let the camp open."

Sharyn hung up the phone and put her head in her hands. She was exasperated. She understood the need for state money in the quickly-growing area, but they were risking so much by agreeing to go ahead. Of course, she couldn't prove that the killer would kill again or even if he or she was still out there. But if the cabin falling down on her hadn't been an accident, he or she was willing to hurt her or kill her to keep the secret. That worried her. What if one of the children accidentally stumbled onto some other secret? The chances for something terrible happening were too great.

"Line two," Trudy told her, looking around the doorway. "Ms. Madison-Farmer returning your call."

"Thanks," Sharyn said, picking up the phone.

"Sheriff Howard, if you think you can influence

me on this charge against your aunt, I can tell you now that I won't be bribed!"

"I wouldn't think of it, Ms. Madison-Farmer. In fact, I'd like to hire you myself. I've been doing some research on historical properties and I need your advice. Are you free for lunch?"

"Is this a trick?" the other woman asked.

"No," Sharyn assured her. "I'm very serious. Lunch?"

"All right. Are you buying?"

"Do you ask all your prospective clients that?"

"Only the ones I'm pretty sure are going to waste my time."

"If it's a waste of your time," Sharyn confirmed, "then lunch is on me."

"Great. I'll meet you at twelve-thirty at the coffee shop across the street. I'll only have about thirty minutes, so please be brief!"

Sharyn shook her head as she hung up the phone. It might have been easier driving around than talking with people on the phone. Her knee might not hurt, but she was getting an incredible headache.

"Bingo!" Cari said, running into her office. "Sheriff, I found something!"

"Something helpful?"

"I think so. I found Betsy Peterson's aunt. Her name is Carmella Peterson. She lives in Gold Hill. I think she's still alive."

"Great! Do we have a phone number for her?"

"Here it is." Cari produced it with a flourish. "Deputy Watkins was right. You *can* find strange things on the computer."

"Do we have any friends yet for Betsy?"

"Not yet."

"Okay. I'll call Ms. Peterson, and you see if you can find any friends."

"Thanks, Sheriff."

Nick knocked on the door, moving aside as Cari ran past him. "I'm going out for an early lunch. What are you doing about lunch? And don't tell me that you're not eating!"

"I have an appointment for lunch," she told him.

"Work related?" he wondered.

"No. Personal."

He nodded. "I guess I'll see you later then."

"Okay."

Nick passed Ernie on his way out of the building.

"How's she doing?" Ernie asked with a nod at Sharyn's office.

"She looked a little pale. Her knee probably hurts. And I kissed her last night." He took a deep breath.

"What?"

Nick glanced uneasily around them in the noisy office. "Which part didn't you understand?"

Ernie grinned. "It wasn't that I didn't understand,

Nick, you old dog! You finally worked your way up to something?"

"It wasn't like that," Nick whispered. "I don't even know if she remembers it."

"Want me to ask her?" Ernie volunteered with mischief in his eyes.

"No!"

"Nick, you're too old for these games," Ernie admonished.

"You're telling me. She wouldn't go out for lunch with me. She said it was something personal."

"Maybe it was."

"Could you…" He paused. "Could you notice if she does go out for lunch? Maybe you could ask her out for lunch. If she won't go out with you either then we'll know it really was something personal and not because she remembers that I kissed her and she doesn't want to be alone with me again."

"Slow down, old son! You're gonna give yourself a coronary like that! I'll see if I can find out what's going on."

Nick shrugged. "Not that it matters about her going out with me for lunch. I just want to make sure she eats. You know."

"Yeah." Ernie grinned and pushed up his glasses. "I know."

Nick shrugged into his coat and left the office.

"What's his problem?" Trudy asked, coming to give Ernie a message.

"He kissed her, Trudy."

Trudy smiled wide. "I think you owe me five dollars, Deputy!"

"But he thinks she might not remember. It was after the accident."

"Doesn't matter. He still kissed her. Pay up!"

Ernie produced a five-dollar bill from his pocket, then walked into Sharyn's office. "Busy?" he asked her.

"Frustrated," she replied. "They won't stop the camp from opening this weekend, Ernie. Tomorrow morning, those buses are going to be rolling in. I can't stop them."

He took a seat. "I guess we'll just have to patrol the camp. It only lasts two weeks and there's gonna be plenty of people out there. I don't think anyone will try anything while it's going on."

"Since this doesn't make much sense so far, we can't assume that it's the product of a sane mind."

"Well, we're on the right track now anyway," he assured her. "I found her birth certificate. Elizabeth Jane Peterson. She matches the initials."

"But where is she, Ernie?"

"I don't know yet. I did line up an interview with a close friend of hers, though. Brian Mason. He was her boyfriend at one time. He was at the college at the same time as her. They were steady together through their senior year. According to the yearbook, the senior class voted them the couple most likely to have five kids together."

"Great! I've got an interview with her aunt, Carmella Peterson. She's out at the nursing home where your father was."

"We can drive out together, then," Ernie said. "What are you doing for lunch? We could catch something to eat, then go out after."

Sharyn glanced at her watch then got stiffly to her feet. "I can't, Ernie. I have lunch with someone else and I better hobble on over now or I'll be late. It shouldn't take long. We can meet back here by one-thirty and go from there. Okay?"

"Sounds good. Anything I can help with?"

"No, thanks, Ernie. It's a personal matter."

"How are you feeling after last night?" he asked her.

"I'm all right. Sore and hurt, but all right. Thanks for asking."

"But—" he stopped her again "—how are you doing, with everything that happened and all?"

She smiled. "I'm fine, Ernie. Quit clucking over me like a mother hen!"

"Any memory loss or any other sign of head trauma?"

Sharyn frowned. "I think my brain is intact,

Ernie. Is there a problem? Do I have my clothes on backwards or something?"

"No," he relented, not wanting to give himself away. "No. I was just wondering."

"I'm fine. Really. Now I have to go to lunch or I'll be late!"

"See you after lunch. I'll bring the car around front so you don't have to walk so far."

"Thanks."

When she was gone, he collapsed on her desk.

"Did you ask her?" Trudy asked, finding him there.

"No! And I'm not going to ask her. She deserves some privacy."

Trudy looked skeptical. "You mean you're afraid she'll take your head off if you start getting into her private life?"

"I'm going to lunch, Trudy," he told her. "I'm taking the sheriff out afterwards for two interviews. We probably won't be back until close to four or five."

"So you have plenty of time to pump her for information without her being suspicious?"

He grinned. "Exactly!"

SELMA HOWARD HEARD the knock on her front door and went to look out of the window. There was a black limousine parked in her driveway. She didn't think it was from the highway department. She dried her hands on her apron and answered the door.

"Jack!"

"Selma," he answered with a smile. "As beautiful as ever." He handed her a bouquet of wildflowers. "I thought you'd like these better than the tame ones."

"Thank you," she responded. "What brings you all the way out here?"

"Can I come in? The wind is a little cool today."

Selma pursed her lips. She knew he was going to want to come in and sit down to come to the point. "I thought we agreed that it was better for you not to come here."

He walked in and she closed the door behind him. "I know where Sharyn is. Did you offer her the...opportunity...to help you?"

"Yes, I did," she answered. "She declined."

He rested his hand on the banister at the base of the stairs. "I don't think you tried very hard, Selma."

"Believe what you like, Jack. She didn't play *your* game to get me out of jail either!"

Jack Winter laughed smoothly. "Don't make it sound like a great thing, Selma. People who can't bend sometimes get blown over."

"That's true enough. But I won't help you again. Sharyn does things her own way."

He nodded his gray head. "*That's* true enough. I've had my dealings with her."

Selma looked at him. He was as smooth and as slippery as an eel. "I don't know how you corrupted my brother, Jack. I don't want to know. But I don't owe you a thing now. We're even. I won't help you corrupt my niece."

"You're as tactful as ever, Selma."

"Thank you. Now don't insult me anymore and get off of my property."

"You act like I want to hurt her," he replied with a voice like dark velvet. "I want to recruit Sharyn to my office. She's wasted in the sheriff's office. I want her to work as the A.D.A. She's clever and ambitious and resourceful."

Selma leveled him a knowing look. "Aren't you afraid she might want *your* job then, Jack?" He smiled again and glanced at the gleaming hardwood floors beneath his feet. "I'm planning to move on anyway. I think I've been D.A. of Montgomery County for long enough. Don't you?"

"You're a wicked man, Jack Winter. You always have been. You asked me out once on a date, do you remember?"

He frowned. "Yes, I do."

"Then you know what my answer is to this piece of tomfoolery. I did this one thing for you because of that business with you and T. Raymond. I won't help you again. Sharyn will make up her own mind. She's too good for you, and that's why you want her somewhere you can control her. I won't be part of it!"

Jack Winter smoothed his hand down the sweet patina of the wood banister and looked up at the sweep of the stairs. "This is a beautiful house, Selma. It will be a shame to see it in pieces with a road where it used to be."

"Don't pretend you have any influence over that, Jack! And give me that note you promised before you go."

He smiled and handed her the folded note from his pocket.

Selma slammed the door behind Jack Winter's retreating form. She was furious, but she was also terrified. She felt faint for a moment and had to hold her head down between her knees. Then she got up and trashed the flowers he'd brought her. She looked at the note he'd given her then lit it on fire with the flame from the gas stove. She made a cup of lemon balm tea for her nerves and sat down at her kitchen table to drink it. She could never tell Sharyn the truth.

BRIAN MASON WAS a thick man in his forties with a football player's neck and the waistline of the in-surance salesman he'd become since taking over his father's business after college. He was effusive in his greeting when he met Sharyn and Ernie, and pressed business cards into both their hands.

"I was surprised that you called about Betsy," he told them. "I haven't thought about her in years. Is she in trouble?"

"We don't really know, Mr. Mason," Sharyn told him. "We're trying to locate her."

"I haven't seen her since that first year of college. We started out together but she met someone else and that was that."

"Who did she meet?" Ernie asked.

"I didn't know him. He wasn't part of our crowd. She never introduced us to him, and we all just drifted apart after that. Mike and I still have a few beers now and again, but otherwise, the group separated. You know, it happens after college."

"So you don't have any idea who the other man was that she left you for?" Sharyn asked again.

"No. But her friend, Heather, might. They go way back. I think they went to grammar school together. She still lives near here. I carry her car insurance for her. Hold on and I'll look up her address."

When he left the room, Sharyn glanced at Ernie. "That was pretty pat."

"He strikes me as the kind of man whose life isn't all that complicated."

Brian Mason returned with a file in his hand. "I have her number at work and home, if you'd like it. If anyone is still in touch with Betsy, it's Heather."

"Thanks, Mr. Mason," Sharyn said, taking the card back from him after he'd written down Heather's numbers. "You act like it wasn't a big deal that Betsy left you for someone else after the two of you were so tight in high school."

Brian shrugged his broad shoulders. "I've been married and divorced three times, Sheriff, and I'm working on number four." His secretary smiled as she walked in and out of the room. "Believe me, the hurt gets less each time it happens. I remember being upset when Betsy left me. But I had my whole life in front of me. I was more upset when my second wife got the Mercedes."

Sharyn and Ernie thanked him, then left his office. They got back in the sheriff's car and headed to the rest home where Carmella Peterson lived.

"He's younger than me and he's already been married three times," Ernie said with a shrug.

"No wonder he's cynical about relationships."

"They work sometimes," Ernie remarked.

"You and Annie seem to be working."

"That's true. And your daddy loved your mama until the day he died. There was never another woman for him. I always wanted what they had together."

Sharyn took out the two numbers Brian had given her. "I'm going to call Heather Dougherty and see if she knows what happened to Betsy."

"What about you?" Ernie tried to turn the conversation. "Aren't you interested in having a relationship like your mama and daddy?"

"No!" She shuddered. "I'd rather live alone my whole life."

She started dialing the first number. Ernie took the hint and let the subject drop.

THE RETIREMENT HOME brought back a lot of painful memories for Ernie. His father had died there a year ago. They had never been close, but it was terrible watching him deteriorate with Alzheimer's disease. He had finally become a shell of the man Ernie remembered, leaving Ernie and his mother to make do the best they could. He had never forgiven his father. Ernie pitied Keith and Paul Reynolds, having to watch Ezekiel die that way.

Carmella Peterson was another story. She was cheerful and able to get around on her own. Her hands were knotted with arthritis but she smiled and welcomed them to her home. "It's good to see a friendly face. I don't have any relatives nearby, but I make friends easily, and the people here have become my family."

"We're looking for someone who is a part of

your family, Ms. Peterson," Ernie told her. "Your niece, Betsy."

"Betsy? Oh, I haven't seen or heard from her for years. I don't even know where she went."

"When was the last time you saw her?" Sharyn asked.

"Oh, that's easy. It was about a month after she had the baby."

"Baby?"

"Yes. I wouldn't talk about it for a long time. I never even told her father, because I promised her that I wouldn't tell him. He was a volatile man. He was my brother and I loved him, but he had a terrible temper. I never knew what he might do next! When she told me that she was pregnant, we both knew it was going to mean trouble if he found out. He beat his poor wife into an early grave. He was just as likely to kill Betsy if he found out she was pregnant. He wanted her to finish school."

"But she had the baby?" Ernie asked.

"Oh, yes. She came to stay with me when she couldn't hide it anymore."

"When was that, ma'am?"

"Probably the last three months before the baby was born. Twenty-five years now. She dropped out of school. She was terrified that her father might find out somehow. I was, too. He was so unpredictable, you see. She told him that she was staying with me because of a special project she was doing for school. Gold Hill is closer to Diamond Springs than Indian Creek so he went along with it."

"When did she have the baby?"

"On a late night in early May. I can't quite recall the date. It was a boy. I do remember that. He was strong and healthy. She was so proud of him, but we weren't sure what to do. Every time a car went by, we were afraid it was Melvin, her father. I was so worried, I was sick! Ulcers. I was always a little delicate after my first husband died."

Sharyn looked at the woman. "What did you do?"

"Well, we knew we couldn't support the baby on my late husband's pension that I lived on at the time, so we went to Social Services for help. They wanted to know the daddy's name, and Betsy didn't want to tell them. She was afraid for him if Melvin found out. She took their help while she was recovering from the birth, but then she was going to go out and get a job."

"Did she?"

"There was one other complication. She had signed on to be a counselor at a camp for poor children at Bell's Creek. They were going to pay her, although it wasn't much. Mostly, I think she wanted to do it because she wanted to be a girl again for a couple of weeks. Carefree and single, you know?

I agreed to take care of the baby until she came back. But she never came back. I thought it went to her head and she couldn't take up her responsibilities again."

"And the child?" Ernie questioned.

"He was so wonderful, but I just couldn't care for him. Social Services wouldn't help me because I didn't know where his real mother and father were. I loved him like my own but I didn't want him to starve to death. I wanted him to have a good life."

"So you gave him up for adoption," Sharyn guessed.

"Yes, ma'am. I took him to a home for foundlings. I cried for days. I never saw him again. I've thought about him plenty over the years. I've thought about Betsy, too, especially when her daddy died. There might have been something else to do, but at the time, I didn't know what it was. I did the best I could."

"I'm sure you did, ma'am." Sharyn consoled her with a smile. "Did your niece give the baby a name? Something we can check with Social Services?"

"She called him Willy Peterson. She never would admit who the daddy was or tell him about the baby. She just kept saying he wouldn't want to know. Do you have some idea of where she went, Sheriff?"

Sharyn touched the older woman's cool hand.

"I think she might not have left on her own, ma'am. I think someone may have forced her to leave."

"Oh, my!"

"Do you remember hearing about the murder at Bell's Creek campground, ma'am?" Ernie asked gently.

"Yes." She looked at Sharyn and Ernie. "But that girl who was killed was a child. Betsy was already a young woman. She wasn't the girl who was killed."

"No, ma'am. But we found a suitcase with some of Betsy's things in it. We also found her purse. There was a note inside that sounded a lot like she was going to go away secretly. But we think she might have been killed."

Carmella's brown eyes filled with tears. "I should have known. All those years being angry with her. Betsy wouldn't have left the baby and me alone. Not if she had a choice."

"What did you tell her father when she left?" Ernie asked.

"I told him that she had run off with a boy. I thought he'd be furious, but he was just sort of re-signed to it. Like he wasn't surprised. I didn't tell him about the baby, though. I thought he might try to harm him if he knew. As I said, Melvin had a temper and you never knew what was going to rile him. I thought he'd be screaming and break-ing things when I told him about Betsy. Instead, he seemed happier that he wasn't going to have to pay for her to go to college anymore. I never understood his moods."

"Thank you so much for your time, Ms. Peterson. If we find out anything for sure about Betsy, we'll let you know."

"Just one more thing," Sharyn interrupted Ernie. "Was your brother left- or right-handed?"

Carmella smiled sweetly, with all the lost knowledge of the past in her eyes. "He was a southpaw, like our daddy before him. People said that's why he got the terrible temper because our daddy had one, too. But Melvin was worse. Bless his soul."

Sharyn and Ernie left the old lady in the sunroom and got back in the car.

"Think there's any reason to go and see the girlfriend?" Ernie asked.

"I don't know."

"It sounds to me like the girl's daddy might have found out the girl was pregnant and tried to take care of the problem, not realizing that she'd already had the baby."

"I'd like something a little more to corroborate it before we say Melvin Peterson was a murderer."

Ernie shrugged as he started the car. "It all fits together. Nick's friend said a left-handed man wrote the note. He got her to go out there by herself and he killed her. No telling where he put her body. That's why he wasn't surprised when his sister told him the girl was gone. He knew right where she was."

"But he wouldn't have had any reason to kill off the other girl," Sharyn pointed out.

"Unless he thought he could hide it that way. After all, here we are twenty-five years later and no one thought to look for Betsy before now. If it was a diversion, it worked."

"We have no way of knowing if Betsy was dead before or after Rebecca Liston was found."

"Maybe that was the beauty of the plan," Ernie theorized. "He killed his daughter, realized what he did, then hid her body and killed the other girl to cover for it. The next day, the campground emptied out faster than water from a sieve. He went in and disposed of Betsy's body. Because of the circumstances, no one missed her until now."

"Maybe you're right," Sharyn agreed. "I wish we had something more to show for it. And if Melvin killed the two girls, who pushed the roof down on me?"

EIGHT

"I went for a ride with my son today. We went up to talk to one of the counselors at the camp who lives in Charlotte. She didn't have much to say, the horror of it being too fresh in her mind. It was the drive with my son that was most remarkable. I finally realized that he has become a man. I'm proud of him. I would like to see him take my place with this badge on his chest."

SHARYN LOOKED UP from her grandfather's journal. Would her father have felt the same way about *her*, if he'd had the chance? Or would he have been just as shocked and horrified as her mother that she was wearing his badge? She glanced at the time and realized that she would have to get going. She wanted to be out at the campground when the buses rolled in that morning.

The state had decided it didn't like the connotations of calling the camp Bell's Creek campground again. So, a member of the statehouse opted to call it Camp Sunshine. Camp Sunshine opened bright and early Saturday morning for the first busloads of noisy children. Reporters from local and national media crowded around. The governor was there for the first bus to roll through. He smiled as the first child walked off the bus. They took his picture, then he was gone in his limousine.

The county commission had coerced the state into having a few security guards for the weekend, just to make sure that everything was running smoothly. Kristie and Keith had rounded up a group of college students and one faculty advisor who would be responsible for the children.

If the pilot project worked, the state would be starting two-week camps for underprivileged youngsters all across the state. If it didn't, it was good P.R. for the people involved who were running for election.

Caison Talbot was out there in his familiar white suit to welcome the children and smile for the cameras. He made polite statements about how important the children of North Carolina were to the future. Sharyn watched his posturing as he walked through the camp with her mother hanging on his arm and his every word. She turned away and shook her head.

"He's more interested in the photo op than the kids," Kristie said, approaching her sister. "How are you feeling? I haven't seen you since you got out of the hospital."

"I'm fine," Sharyn replied, still hobbling on her hurt knee. "The stitches come out Monday. I'll be good as new."

"But you're still not sure about the camp, are you?"

Sharyn looked at her pretty younger sister. Kristie had the looks and a life that many girls would envy. She thought about that other girl, Elizabeth Peterson, who seemed to have it all going for her as well. "I don't want to argue with you anymore about this."

"I don't want to argue with you either," her sister confessed, hugging her. "When I heard that you were hurt and saw them taking you out of that cabin, I was sick! We could've had that argument and you could've died without us making up. I don't ever want to have that happen again. Okay?"

Sharyn hugged her sister. "I agree."

Kristie looked at the kids, who were eagerly finding their cabins. The sounds of their laughter and their excited talk filled the hollow silence that usually encompassed the area. "But you still feel we shouldn't have opened?"

"I don't know, Kristie," Sharyn admitted. "We still don't know what happened out here. I wish I had something more than just a man who might have killed someone who's not here to defend himself. I'd like to know if someone cut those beams in cabin five. But I'm starting to feel as hopeless about it as Grandpa."

"I understand what you're saying," Kristie agreed. "But look at them! Look how much they're enjoying this! Isn't it worth the risk?"

"I hope so. I'm going to have a deputy drive by through here a few times a day. You'll have the security guards patrolling for the first two days." Sharyn put her hands on her sister's arms and looked into her face. "But if you have any trouble or notice anything out of the ordinary, call for help. Don't wait. I don't care if it seems silly. Make sure you tell someone. Don't take any chances. All right?"

Kristie didn't know if she had ever seen so much worry etched on Sharyn's face. "All right. It's gonna be okay, Sharyn. Relax. The place has a bad rep, that's all. It'll be fine."

"Where's Keith?" Sharyn asked. Another girl, who could have been Kristie's twin, bounced up to them with a clipboard of names and information.

"I haven't seen him yet this morning," Kristie admitted. "He was supposed to be here. I talked to him last night but he sounded strange."

"I thought I saw Keith down by the kitchen," the

other girl, Amber, volunteered with a bright smile. "He was chasing that weird old guy."

"Must be his grandfather," Kristie said. "Amber, this is my sister, Sharyn. She's the sheriff of this county."

"Wow! Awesome job," Amber told her. Her blue eyes looked the uniform up and down and she frowned. "I think you should have them re-design the uniforms though."

"Thanks," Sharyn said with a smile. "Kristie, be careful. I'll talk to you later."

Ernie joined her as she was walking back to her Jeep. "I think there might be more reporters and candidates here than children."

"Good. The more people, the less chance we're going to have any problems." She turned to him as she got in the Jeep. "Ernie, what did you find out about Keith Reynolds?"

As she mentioned him, Keith's face appeared outside the Jeep window. "Hi, Sheriff. I was wondering if you could give me a hand. My dad and I are trying to get my grandfather home."

"Sure thing," Sharyn replied. "Ernie has some experience in this."

Ernie nodded. "You're gonna have to put him somewhere for his own safety, son."

"I know," Keith agreed. "My dad doesn't want

to do it but we can't watch him all the time. He's getting worse."

Ernie and Sharyn joined the search for the man. Sharyn called in the helicopter an hour later as the sun rose higher and the day began to warm. There was still no sign of Ezekiel Reynolds. She saw Paul Reynolds standing at the side of the creek, looking into its dark, foaming depths.

"I've called in some help," she told him.

"We don't need it," he replied caustically. "We can help our own."

"He's disappeared, Mr. Reynolds," Sharyn reminded him, holding on to her patience. "He could fall into this creek and drown. A car could hit him in the road. He has to be found and put somewhere where he can be protected from himself."

He turned to her. "What do you know about it, Sheriff? Have you ever had to do something that racked your soul because you loved another human being so much but you knew it had to be done?"

Sharyn studied him, her eyes narrowed on his face. "I think I have, sir. Have *you?*"

Paul Reynolds glared at her but before he could speak, there was a shout from another part of the campground. Keith and Ernie had found Ezekiel.

"I'm afraid I'm going to have to insist that you take more serious steps to help your father, sir."

The pastor looked back at her. "We'll take care of our own, Sheriff. Like we've always done."

Sharyn started to speak again, then thought better of it. The man was already agitated. She didn't need to make it any worse right now. She'd have someone from Social Services check on it tomorrow and see what his response had been to her directive. He walked away quickly. Sharyn followed more slowly behind him.

Ernie started up the Jeep when she joined him. He waved to J.P. as the young deputy did a first patrol through the campground before going home from the night shift. "Not a whole lot to tell about Keith Reynolds. We already know his history. He's an adopted preacher's son. He did okay in school but nothing to get any awards. He was about the same at State but there were financial difficulties. He didn't transfer to the local college just to be close to Kristie, although that probably figured into it. His tuition was paid late several times. He had late fees on everything. I think he couldn't afford it anymore and had to go to the local school to save money."

"Nick mentioned that part of the problem was the father wanting to keep the grandfather from going to a home. He wants Keith to help him."

Ernie shook his head. "No way. You saw the old guy. He's disoriented, muttering about ghosts and demons and trying to find something he lost. He needs more than they can give him. Keith said he's only in his early sixties. What a waste."

"Kristie says Keith has been acting strange the last day or so. I don't think she understands the strain he's under trying to keep up with everything."

"I hope she never has to understand that strain. I feel for Keith and his father. I didn't really love my daddy but it was hard," Ernie said as they drove back to Diamond Springs.

She looked at him. "Are you satisfied with the idea that it was Betsy Peterson's father who killed her?"

Ernie shrugged. "I'm not happy that we don't have more evidence to prove it. But it's a twenty-five year old case. Even if he were alive, we'd have a tough time proving he did it. We don't have a body. We do know he had opportunity and motive. He could have had an alibi for that night. He had a temper and somehow found out about his daughter getting pregnant. Even his own sister was afraid of him. He was a southpaw and he could have written her that note, waited for her to come out, then killed her and dumped her body anywhere, including the creek."

"Then he killed the little girl to cover it up so no one would look for Betsy," she concluded.

"Yes, ma'am."

"But the only proof we have is his sister's accusations. What about the baby's father? Betsy's aunt said he didn't want the baby," Sharyn considered. "Maybe we should go and have a talk with Heather Dougherty after all."

"What is it that's bothering you about the case?" Ernie asked. "You've got more than your granddaddy ever had on it."

She shook her head and looked out of the window at the fresh spring landscape. "I don't know, Ernie. We're about to ruin a man's name forever. He might be dead, but I'd like something else to corroborate what we have before I close this file."

He glanced at her. "You're just plain, mule stubborn."

Sharyn frowned at him as she dialed Heather's number. "I'm just saying I'd like to know more about Betsy before I let her murder go."

When she had finished setting up an interview with Heather Dougherty, Ernie glanced at her. "If all of this is because of the house falling on you, as one of the investigating officers, I'd say it was a draw about those timbers being cut. I think the cabin just fell in on you. John Schmidt saw it one way. Another expert could see those timbers as rotten."

Sharyn acknowledged that, and realized that it could be true. She'd thought about it while she was having the long line of tests done at the hospital.

"I know. I just want to be sure that whoever murdered those two girls doesn't get away with it for another twenty-five years. I want to feel better about saying Melvin Peterson killed his own daughter."

"Okay." Ernie nodded. "I suppose that note could have been from her real boyfriend as well as her father."

"Maybe Betsy didn't keep the pregnancy as secret as she thought. She said the baby's father wouldn't want it. He might have known she was pregnant, and thought he was taking care of both problems. It was pretty obvious something was wrong with her to make her drop out of school and go to live with her aunt. But she managed to keep the baby a secret."

"Of course, there's nothing but conjecture at this point that could link the two murders."

"But that's a lot of conjecture, Ernie! Two murders, probably on the same night, in the same place. Both girls slashed with a knife."

"But without Betsy's body—"

"We have her dress, even though we don't know why she wasn't in it. According to Nick, she was in it when she was killed. The blade was probably about the same size as the wounds they found in Rebecca's body."

Ernie sighed and turned into the driveway of

the elegant white brick home. "I'm not the D.A. but you've convinced me. Let's talk to Ms. Dougherty."

THEY SAT DOWN IN Heather Dougherty's expensive living room. Her house overlooked Diamond Lake with a wall of floor-to-ceiling windows.

"What can I do for you, Sheriff?" the woman asked. Her hair was still blond, though it owed most of it to artificial means now. Her waistline was as slim as it had been when she'd been a cheerleader at Diamond Springs High School.

"We're here for information about Elizabeth Peterson."

Heather looked puzzled for a moment, and then her face cleared. "Oh, Betsy! I haven't thought about her in years! She took off for parts unknown after all that mess at the campground twenty-five years ago. I haven't seen her since we left that terrible day."

"You mean the day after the murder?" Ernie asked avidly.

"Yes. We were all so stunned! We didn't have time to think about it or do much more than get our things together. It was probably best that way."

"But you saw Betsy that morning when you were getting ready to leave?" Sharyn asked again.

Heather knitted her brow. "Well, as I said, it was really confusing. I'm not sure who I saw that morning. I do know she wasn't on the same bus I was on, but there were other buses."

"But she was at the campground that night?"

"Definitely."

"The two of you were friends," Sharyn persisted. "Didn't you think it was strange when you didn't see her after leaving the camp?"

Heather shrugged her slender shoulders. "To tell you the truth, Betsy was having some problems. There were rumors about her being pregnant when she dropped out of school. I didn't expect to see her at the campground at all. She'd been gone for a few months. When the campground opened, there she was. We talked a little, but she was pretty secretive about everything. It wasn't like her."

"But she never mentioned a baby to you?"

"No. We didn't talk about it, but then again, we had our hands full with all those kids."

"What cabin did Betsy sleep in?"

"We all slept in different cabins. I slept in number twelve. I'm not sure which one Betsy was in. It was wild out there! Every time I think about that poor little girl and the murderer being so close to me, it still makes me shiver. Do you know what happened to Betsy?"

"We think she might have been hurt or forcibly taken from the campground." Sharyn took out a copy of the note. "We found her purse with this note in it."

Heather looked at it. "This could be from her boyfriend. She was real quiet about him. He wasn't from our school. None of us knew him. I think she kept us away from him on purpose, like she was afraid we might laugh at him. Kids can be pretty cruel."

"We know that Betsy was pregnant. Do you know who the father was?" Ernie wondered.

Heather shrugged. "It wasn't Brian. That's who Betsy was seeing before she met this new guy. Betsy and him were already broken up for too long before we heard the stories about her being pregnant."

"Can you recall anything about the boy she was dating?" Sharyn asked.

Heather frowned and considered the question. "I know that he didn't have much money. I know he didn't have a car because Betsy was always driving him places. He had to be a geek of some kind. He wasn't someone she was proud of and wanted to show off to the rest of us. And she started acting different after they started going out. She didn't drink anymore. She quit smoking and started wearing those long dresses girls were wearing back then. She had great legs and she always loved short skirts. She stopped swearing."

"So, she could have been dating…a seminary student?" Sharyn wondered.

Heather smiled. "It's possible. I couldn't swear to it, but that sounds likely. Sorry I can't be more help."

"It's been a long time," Ernie replied as they took their leave. "If you think of anything else, please give us a call."

"All right." She took his card. "I hope you find out what happened to Betsy."

"Thank you, ma'am." Sharyn took her outstretched hand. "I hope so, too."

"What was that all about?" Ernie asked as they walked out of the house together.

"Keith's father may have been home from school the week the murder happened at the campground."

"So you're thinking—"

"Let's see if we can get enough information about the baby Betsy had without having to try to get the adoption files opened."

Ernie's eyes widened. "You think Keith is Betsy's baby?"

"It seems possible to me." She grinned at him. "Unless you think it's just my mild concussion talking."

Ernie laughed. "I think it could fit in with the attack on you at the campground, but unless you can get him to confess, even if he *is* the father, he would have had the same motivation as Betsy's father, without the evil temper to go with it. That still leaves the whole thing open to interpretation."

"Then I guess we better hope he's been aching to confess for twenty-five years."

"Yeah, that's gonna happen!"

They drove back to the office. Ernie jumped on the computer, since Cari didn't work weekends. Joe walked in, covered in mud. Ed came in after him.

"What have you been doing?" Trudy asked, looking at the pair.

"Well, Joe thought he might like to try riding that cow out in Harmony," Ed told her.

"I ticketed the man for that cow running loose again," Joe told Sharyn. "We've got to have stricter laws for animals running loose. Especially if we have to catch them with our bare hands!"

"You should have seen him!" Ed laughed out loud.

"I needed a tranquilizer gun!"

"You can't tranquilize a cow," Ed told him. "How would you move it?"

"Forklift," Ed replied as he walked into the locker room and slammed the door.

"There's a mess out on the Interstate," Trudy told Ed. "State patrol found a car with drugs. They want someone up there from the county."

"I'm on my way," Ed replied with a nod at Sharyn. "At least it's not catching cows!"

"Take a spin past the campground on your way back," Sharyn advised him.

"Will do, Sheriff."

"How's the leg?" Trudy asked when he had gone.

"Pretty good," Sharyn replied.

Trudy looked at her curiously. "How's the head? Ernie said you were whacked pretty hard."

"It was only a small concussion," Sharyn replied. "Is it something I'm saying or doing that makes everyone worry about my head?"

Trudy smiled. "I'm sure we aren't, Sheriff. We all know how hard-headed you are!"

"Then why—"

"I just thought you might have remembered something else…about what happened. I mean, something you might not remember about the whole thing."

"What?"

Ernie came out of his office and glared at Trudy. "Sheriff, I got that information from the hospital. The baby's blood type was O positive, like the mother. Paul Reynolds had surgery a few years ago. He has type O positive, too."

"So does half the world," Trudy declared, glaring back at him.

"We'd have to have DNA tests done for Mr. Reynolds and Keith."

"Which still won't prove he murdered the girl, so there wouldn't be much hope of having that ordered by the court."

"Exactly."

Sharyn limped to her office. "I think we should go and talk to the pastor again. Give me a minute and I'll be right with you."

When she was gone, Ernie leaned down close to Trudy's face. "You're gonna give the whole thing away!"

"You didn't find out anything yesterday. I thought I might as well try."

"If she finds out—"

"Are you saying I can't find out without her guessing that I know?"

"Ready." Sharyn looked between Ernie and Trudy. "Is something wrong?"

"No."

"No," Ernie echoed. He cleared his throat.

Sharyn sighed. "I'm glad it's not my birthday."

"Why?"

"Because the two of you look like you're planning a surprise party or something. Ready, Ernie?"

"Ready, Sheriff."

They found Paul Reynolds praying in the church sanctuary. The church was dark around him. Only the sunlight, streaming through the stained-glass images of Moses and the crucifixion, illuminated him. His hands were clasped before him and his head was bowed.

"Pastor Reynolds?" Ernie approached him, more mindful than usual of the man's calling.

Paul Reynolds didn't turn around to face them. "I'm sending my father away. Is there anything else, Sheriff?"

"Yes, sir," she answered. "I'm afraid there is."

He turned to them. His eyes were wild and his face was wet with tears. "What now?"

"It's about your son, sir."

"Keith?"

Sharyn stared hard at him. "Is he your son, sir? Your real son?"

He shook his head. "Are you accusing me of being a bad father now, Sheriff? Is that it? Is this because he can't be at that other school?"

Ernie stepped in. "No, sir. We aren't accusing you of anything. We're looking for information. We think we finally know what happened to Elizabeth Peterson."

"Elizabeth Peterson?" He looked at them both. "Should I know that name?"

"Well, that's where the problem comes in, sir. You see, some people think you might have been the father of her baby. We talked to her aunt. She tells

JOYCE & JIM LAVENE

us that Elizabeth didn't want to tell the father that she was pregnant because she said he didn't want the baby. But she had the baby anyway. We were wondering if that baby might be Keith."

"You're telling me that this Elizabeth Peterson was pregnant and she said the father wouldn't want the baby? Then you're telling me that you think I'm the father and I adopted him? I don't think that makes any sense, Deputy."

"We'd appreciate knowing the name of the orphanage where you adopted Keith," Sharyn told him. "We'd appreciate it even more if you would volunteer to have a DNA test to prove if you are Keith's natural father."

"I will not!" Paul Reynolds thundered. "I adopted Keith. The orphanage was closing. He wasn't the only child there. They needed help placing them all. You can't prove any of this, or you wouldn't be *asking* for a test!"

"That may be true, right now," Ernie agreed. "But we can get a court order for this."

"On what grounds?"

"On the grounds that we believe Elizabeth Peterson was murdered and it's possible that the baby's father would have had a reason for killing her, if he thought she was still pregnant and didn't realize she'd already had the baby."

"Murdered?" The pastor could barely say the word. "Murdered? What proof do you have?"

Sharyn nodded. It was obvious to her that Paul Reynolds knew who Betsy was. "I think we should continue this discussion at the sheriff's office, sir."

"I've done nothing wrong!" he defended himself. "You can't arrest me for a suspicion!"

"We're not arresting you, sir," Ernie replied calmly. "Just asking you to come to the office with us."

The pastor looked at them both as though he were about to hurl something their way. Then his rage seemed to pass. "Very well. But I'll call my lawyer."

"That's fine, sir," Ernie told him. "We'll be sure you have a ride back from the office."

"Sorry to inconvenience you, Mr. Reynolds," Sharyn said. "But we have to get to the truth on this."

They drove to the office in stony silence. Sharyn watched as Ernie seated the man at the conference table, then she went into her office to call the D.A. They were going to need a court order for that DNA test. To her surprise, about twenty minutes later, Jack Winter showed up. Carefully dressed in a gray suit with a wine-colored tie, he removed his overcoat and gave it to Trudy, telling her that he wanted a cup of coffee.

Trudy started to throw his coat back at him, but Sharyn quickly grabbed it from her. Chastened, she slunk to the coffee machine to make Jack Winter a cup of coffee.

"Well, Sharyn," Jack started, smiling at her. "You never come to see me anymore, so I thought I should come to see you. What's all this about?"

She filled him in as Trudy handed him a cup of coffee. He looked at the foam cup, then shrugged and sipped from it.

"We're waiting for Jeff Richards to get here," Sharyn advised him.

"Why?" Jack asked her. "If the man wants to confess, he doesn't need a lawyer."

"He doesn't want to confess," she explained.

Jack shrugged again and tossed away his coffee. "I don't think you have to worry about it with me here to protect your reputation, Sharyn." He made a face. "I do think you should take some of that new money from the commission and get a decent coffee pot!"

"But—"

He put his finger against Sharyn's mouth and leaned his head close to hers. Nick walked in at that moment, and Trudy felt goose bumps jump up and down her spine.

"We'll be fine," Jack assured Sharyn. "Are you ready?"

Sharyn jerked her head back from Jack's touch against her skin. "After you, sir."

Jack smiled, then led her into the conference room that also doubled as the interrogation room. Sharyn called one of their weekend volunteers in to write up Paul Reynolds' statement. She didn't see Nick as she closed the door behind them.

"What was that all about?" Nick asked Trudy, putting his gloves in his coat pocket.

"Just the special relationship the Sheriff has with the D.A.," she replied with a smile. "Tell me about the kiss, Nick?"

Nick groaned. "I shouldn't have told Ernie."

"I'm not telling anyone else!" Trudy protested. "Just share the details."

"I think the phone is ringing, Trudy."

"Those are bells, Nick," she explained to him patiently. "You'll be hearing a lot of them now."

"Trudy!" He glared at her, but she only smiled sweetly at him. "Just tell her I was here. I'll call later. What's up, anyway?"

"They picked up Paul Reynolds to talk to him about being Keith's biological father and possibly the Peterson girl's killer."

"Pastor Reynolds?"

"You didn't know? The sheriff thinks he's the baby's father and that he might have killed Eliza-beth Peterson because he thought she was still pregnant. He came to find out later that she'd had the child, and then Pastor Reynolds adopted him."

"And he's here to confess to that?"

Trudy grimaced. "Not exactly. I think they're hoping for a miracle."

Nick looked at the closed door. "I might have something to contribute then. I took some prints from that wood that was cut at the cabin. And I have another partial from the note."

"Do they belong to Paul Reynolds?" Trudy asked.

Nick shrugged. "I don't know. I didn't know they were going that way with the investigation. When they take his prints, we should know."

Trudy grinned wickedly. "I think you should go in there and tell them, then."

Nick smiled back. "I think you're right. Thanks."

They had just gotten set up to take Paul Reynolds' statement when Nick leaned his head around the door. "Sharyn? Can I talk to you a minute?"

"We're trying to take a man's statement here, Dr. Thomopolis," Jack Winter reminded him.

Ernie glanced up at Nick's dark face. "I'm sure Nick wouldn't be here if he didn't have something important to contribute."

"I'm glad you have confidence in that, Deputy Watkins." The D.A. stood up slowly as Sharyn stood up. "I guess you might as well tell me your urgent news, Dr. Thomopolis, and save Sharyn from having to relay it to me."

"This is department news," Nick told him bluntly.

"Technically, I'm the head of the department," Jack said smoothly.

"Then it's *private* department news," Nick snarled.

"Oh, it's private? Well, then by all means, take your time, Sheriff. We're only trying to solve a murder that happened twenty years ago. A few more minutes for your personal life won't matter."

He sat back down. Sharyn frowned as she walked out of the room and closed the door behind her. "What's up?"

"I had John bring me some of those pieces of wood that fell on you. I found a few good prints, all from the same person. I also lifted a partial print from that note."

"Any matches?"

"Nothing that I could find. Whoever it is doesn't have a police or service record."

She nodded. "That might take Melvin Peterson, Betsy's father, off the list. His sister said he was in the Army. If that print on the note had been his, we would have had some solid evidence."

"I'll check him out." He wrote down the name. "But if you think he killed his daughter and the Liston girl, why do you have Paul Reynolds here?"

"Because he's the only other person we have to

look at. I'm going to try to get a DNA test done on Paul and Keith. Maybe I can swing some fingerprints, too. Get me something concrete besides speculation and innuendo. I'd like to put this away."

"For the record, I think those beams were cut to fall on you. I think whoever did it was either the killer or someone trying to protect the killer."

She glanced in the conference room. "Thanks, Nick. This can be my ace-in-the-hole, if I need it."

"You're welcome. Let me know what happens."

"I will." She disappeared behind the door.

Nick was able to glare at Jack Winter again before the door finished closing. "I'm leaving now," he told Trudy. "But that was fun. Someday, someone is going to kill that man."

"I wish I had enough nerve to do it," Trudy declared balefully. "But I'll have to leave him to his Maker."

"I'm sorry, Trudy," Nick said, touching her hand. "We all did what we could. There just wasn't any evidence."

"I know," she replied. "And I'm not bitter. *What goes around, comes around,* my mama always used to say. He'll get his, Nick."

NINE

JEFF RICHARDS HAD agreed to defend Pastor Reynolds. He'd finally shown up and was speaking privately with his new client in the conference room. Ernie and the volunteer taking the statement were waiting outside the door.

"I think I'll be going," Jack Winter said, reaching for his coat as the A.D.A. walked in to take his place.

Sharyn had been purposely ignoring him, reading the paper while he sat across from her. She looked up as he decided to leave. "I'd like to get a DNA test order on Paul Reynolds and his son. And I need his prints."

"Charge him with the crime," the D.A. told her.

"I'd rather not do that." She smiled at the A.D.A., then closed the door to her office with him on the other side. "And what I want won't necessarily prove he's part of this murder investigation."

Jack nodded, his eyes measuring her face. "And you'd like me to take care of it for you?"

"I know you can have it done in Keith's best interests."

"I could do that," he agreed. "I know a judge who'd do it."

"I'd appreciate it. I don't want this whole thing to blow up in the media before we know the truth."

"And how will you help me in return?"

"What do you want, Mr. Winter?"

He smiled. "Regardless of what you might think of me, Sharyn. I have *your* best interests at heart. I like you."

"But you don't want me to run for sheriff again."

"Exactly. Your best interests aren't served here."

"Are you sure those are *my* best interests?"

"Don't mock me, Sharyn! I feel sure we could work well together in the future. Let's not ruin that."

Sharyn looked at him. His eyes were a pale, flat blue. His voice was calm. There wasn't a hint that he was in any way ruffled by her words. Yet she knew he wasn't just chatting.

"I hope that you aren't threatening me, sir. I believe you wouldn't like to have me as an enemy, any more than I would like to count you among mine."

Jack Winter faltered. She saw it in his eyes. It suddenly occurred to her that she could beat this man at the poker game they had been playing. She hadn't gone to him. He had finally come to her. He wasn't afraid of her, but there was something else. He didn't want her against him either.

The D.A. smiled. It wasn't a happy expression

when combined with his cold eyes. It was more an expression of satisfaction. "You always impress me, Sharyn. That's what I like about you." He surveyed her scratched face. "I suppose doing this small service for you wouldn't be enough to blackmail you into taking the A.D.A. job with my office?"

"No, sir."

"That's what I thought." He sighed. "All right. I'll still get those tests for you, as a sign of good faith between us."

"Thank you, sir."

"Just out of curiosity, what would it take to win you over? Is there a carrot I could dangle in front of you that would take you away from the sheriff's job?"

Sharyn thought about it. "I don't think so, sir. Of course, you can't ever tell what tomorrow will bring."

"Your father used to say that, didn't he? Well, until tomorrow, Sharyn. I know there's a future for us."

"We'll see, sir."

Jack Winter had no sooner left her office than Ernie came in. "Paul Reynolds' lawyer is refusing to let him give blood or let us take his prints unless we formally charge him."

"I think the D.A. will be able to get a court order." She shuffled some papers.

"Sheriff, you wouldn't really, I mean—"

"Join the D.A.'s office?"

"I didn't mean to eavesdrop but these walls are as thin as wax paper."

"I know." She smiled. "I can't imagine myself working for that man, Ernie. You know how I feel about him. Just because I don't antagonize him doesn't mean I like him."

He nodded. "What do you want to do with Pastor Reynolds?"

"We don't really have anything to hold him on right now. Nick is going to need his prints. He has one from the note that was in the pocketbook and one from a roof timber on cabin five. Try to hold him up awhile until we can get that order for the prints and the blood sample."

"Okay. There's just one thing I think you should know," Ernie said.

"What's that?"

"Paul Reynolds writes with his right hand."

"What?"

He nodded. "He wrote everything with his right hand." Sharyn frowned. "Could Nick's handwriting expert be wrong?"

"I don't know. We should ask him."

"I told him I'd let him know how it went anyway, so let's give him a call."

Sharyn explained the situation to Nick, who suggested that they meet with the handwriting expert so that she could form her own opinion on how important it was to the case.

"My office at the college in twenty minutes?"

"Do you keep him in your closet?" she asked lightly.

"No, he's a professor. He teaches handwriting analysis at the college."

"They didn't have classes in that when I went to school."

He laughed. "They did. Handwriting analysis goes back even farther than you!"

Sharyn hung up the phone, then glanced at her watch. "You know, Ernie, it's close enough to quitting time that you could go. I think I can handle Nick and the handwriting expert without too much strain."

"I'd like to go along and hear what he has to say, if you don't mind. Annie and I have this deal. She understands that I get home early when I can and I understand that she doesn't want me to stay late every night."

"Sounds good," Sharyn said. "Let's take the Jeep over to the college. I don't think my knee is up to that walk yet."

Kristie walked into the office as they were signing out. She looked at her sister with frightened eyes. Ernie nodded as Sharyn took her aside.

"Is he…are you going to arrest Keith's dad?"

"I don't know yet," Sharyn told her. "We're waiting for a court order to do a blood sample for a paternity test, and we want to get his fingerprints."

"Mr. Reynolds is *really* Keith's biological father?"

"I don't know yet, Kristie. The evidence is slim."

"But it could be true?"

"It looks that way," Sharyn conceded. "I'm going to check out a few more things, then I'll let you know."

"I'm going to talk to Keith," Kristie explained. "He wanted to be here, but he had to stay with his grandfather. They're going to take him to the hospital for tests. I could hardly get away from the camp. Losing one counselor is bad enough. Losing two would be impossible! I never knew kids could be so difficult."

Ernie joined them. "Makes you appreciate your mama a little more, doesn't it?"

"Yes. It makes me wonder why she had two of us."

Sharyn laughed. "I've wondered that for a long time."

"I guess Mom knew she didn't get it right the first time, huh?" She stuck out her tongue at Sharyn, then sobered. "Thanks, Sharyn. I'll talk to Keith."

"This isn't going to be easy for him to accept."

"I know. I hope you're wrong for once."

"David swung by the camp on his way in, Kristie," Trudy reported from across the room. "He says there's nothing unusual unless you count kids running in the road."

"Thanks, Trudy. That seems to be about normal."

Ernie and Sharyn walked out with Kristie. They met Joe coming in from the street.

"I'd like to call it a day," Joe said. "I'd rather catch a bootlegging, moonshining drug runner than a crazy cow any day!"

"Take it easy, Joe," Sharyn agreed with a laugh. "Ed's got that thing on the Interstate and David and J.P. are on their way in. Tomorrow's your Sunday off anyway, isn't it?"

"You got it!" he agreed. "I'm gonna be mighty glad when we hire some new deputies around here. Maybe I could have a whole weekend off a month."

"Don't go letting those kind of ideas go to your head, son," Ernie suggested.

"Aw, Ernie, we used to not work so hard!"

"You want something easy, you go sell ice cream to the tourists!"

Kristie said good-bye to them. Sharyn considered her sister thoughtfully before she climbed into her Jeep after Ernie. How would all of this affect Kristie? She hadn't been dating Keith long, but she felt that they were pretty close.

"What's up?" Ernie asked, starting the Jeep.

"Just thinking about Kristie in all of this," Sharyn answered. "I hope none of the Reynolds family is involved in this."

THEY MET NICK and his friend at the college a few minutes later. It had started raining lightly, making the early evening dark.

Myron Ollssen was a happy, pink-faced little man with short cinnamon-colored hair and bright blue eyes. He reminded Sharyn of one of Santa's elves. She shook his hand when Nick introduced her, then took a seat at a desk in his classroom.

"Nick has brought me a few examples of handwriting to analyze. As I understand it, these are all people you know, so you'll be familiar with what I'm going to say about them. He didn't give me any names or details. Just examples of their handwriting to work with."

"Yeah, I'm not making it easier for him until he comes down and helps me do an autopsy," Nick quipped.

Myron shuddered. "I wouldn't even consider that! I don't know how you do it for a living, my friend."

Nick raised his hands. "It's all I know how to do."

Myron laughed. "Anyway. I have these samples so that I can show you that handwriting analysis is a science, like forensics. It's not like telling some-one's fortune or being psychic. It's more like fin-gerprint analysis. It's been used for over a hundred years by detectives around the world and the tech-nique is recognized in court as legal evidence." He put on his half-glasses and peered at one set of sen-tences Nick had given him.

"This handwriting belongs to a right-handed man. He slants his *t*'s in an unusual way, so that we know he is forceful and dominant of those around him. He is older, the style and penmanship dem-onstrate that fact. His tastes range to the elegant, but he is hiding something that he does not want the world to see."

"Jack Winter?" Ernie guessed.

Nick looked at the tag. "That's him."

"I say he's secretive because he has a bold stroke but keeps his letters smaller than they need to be," Myron remarked, before taking up another piece of paper. "This is a woman. She's right-handed. She writes like a schoolgirl, suggesting that she is happy where she is. She is resourceful and orderly. You can see the clear loops and careful, legible let-ters. She's cheerful and competent and she deals with stress well."

"Trudy," Sharyn said.

Nick pulled out the answer. "Trudy."

"That's amazing!" Ernie proclaimed.

"Okay, here we have a woman who is trustworthy and dependable. She's resourceful and clever. She's right-handed but her words slant a little to the left, making her fair-minded and open to others' opinions. It wouldn't surprise me for this woman to be in a position of power. But she's also self-sacrificing. She does something a little unique with her *r*'s that place her as being a little rebellious."

"Is she also stubborn? Refuses to be careful in dangerous situations and rarely listens to reason?" Nick wondered. "If so, I think we must have the sheriff of Montgomery County." He opened the flap. "Right on the money!"

"When I was in college and studying this stuff for the first time, it was great at parties. Girls really liked it. I was popular." He looked at Nick. "You should take it up. With your disposition, it might help you get out with a living woman once in a while."

"Thanks, but I don't think so," Nick replied. "I impress my dates with tales of forensic research and looking for murder victims."

Myron waved his hand at him. "Anyway, you get the idea. I have a few cases here on record that will illustrate that some aspects of handwriting are unchangeable."

"Didn't I read once that a schizophrenic could change their handwriting?" Ernie asked.

"That's true," Myron agreed. "But only in one out of a thousand documented studies. And even then, it would be hard to change it completely."

"What about the note Nick had you analyze for this case?" Sharyn asked. "Did you have any doubts about it?"

"Not at all. The handwriting was legible and distinct. Nothing strained about it. It was definitely a left-handed man. His loops are original and his strokes are broad and clear. He knew what he was doing when he wrote that note. He didn't hesitate." He handed Sharyn affidavits of other cases solved or aided by handwriting analysis. "I've testified on cases before. I'd be happy to do so for you, Sheriff Howard."

"Thanks." She shook his hand. "I guess that puts us in a little quandary."

"How's that?" Nick asked.

"Ernie observed Paul Reynolds writing with his right hand."

"Do you have an example?" Myron asked.

Sharyn took out the pastor's signature on a waiver. "What do you think?"

Myron looked at the note and the signature on the document. "No. This is definitely a different man, Sheriff. He's right-handed and not as sure as the first man. His letters are completely different."

"There's been twenty-five years between these

samples," Ernie reminded them. "Maybe they changed with him. A man doesn't stay the same."

"And I don't know if you could call him sane when he wrote this note," Sharyn added. "He was about to kill two people."

Myron looked at the two pages again. "I still feel quite sure this is a different man, Sheriff. Even with age and differences with time, these two signatures aren't alike."

"I guess that's where the real science of forensics takes over," Nick remarked. "All we need is a print from Reynolds and we'll know."

"What about those Melvin Peterson prints?"

Nick shook his head. "I found them. No dice."

Ernie's pager went off. "That's Annie," he said with a lopsided grin. "I'll walk from here." He looked at Nick. "Maybe you could help the sheriff get home?"

"No problem," Nick replied.

"I can get home by myself, thanks," Sharyn told them. "I'll be careful."

"Don't be so stubborn," Ernie admonished, then he shook Dr. Ollssen's hand. "Thanks, Doctor." He nodded to Nick. "She won't give up those Jeep keys easily, you know."

"I know. See you later, Ernie," Nick replied. He glanced at Sharyn. "How about having dinner with me and Myron?"

"Oh, not me," Myron said slowly. "I have a ton of papers to grade before the regular students come back next week. You two go on, though. Have a good time. Maybe you can impress this one with your stories about dead people!"

Sharyn drew in a deep breath. She wanted to go. She didn't want to go. He hadn't mentioned kissing her. Maybe she'd dreamed it. Her memory of that night was pretty foggy. She turned to Myron. "Thanks. Things have a way of working out. If Melvin Peterson or Paul Reynolds aren't the right men, we may have to come back to you for help."

Myron shrugged. "There's no such thing as an exact science."

Nick frowned. "I beg your pardon?"

"There are always possibilities. Good luck anyway."

Sharyn took a deep breath. "Okay. Let's go."

"How's the leg?" Nick asked as she limped out with him.

"Sore," she answered.

"We're only two minutes from that little bar and grill where all the doctors hang out," he said.

"Doctors?" she asked hesitantly.

He shrugged. "I don't mind if you don't. Might make a nice change from cops."

She laughed. "I don't think there can be much of a change when you're having dinner with a cop."

"We could take your Jeep somewhere else." He rubbed his chin. "I've always wanted to drive a Jeep."

"If we take my Jeep, I'll drive," she answered. "You wouldn't trust your Cadillac to my driving."

"True, but you shouldn't be driving until those stitches come out."

"I still have to get home," she reminded him.

"That's true. I guess I'll drive you home in your Jeep."

"Don't push it, Nick."

They managed to get a small table in the crowded grill. It was dark and noisy, but the booth they'd found cut off some of the sound. Doctors and nurses were caterwauling with a karaoke system on the tiny stage. There were dark, wooden blinds at the windows that let in only a small amount of light from the rainy street outside.

"Hey, Doc," the waiter said with a smile. He put down a small plate with herbs and olive oil and another with hot bread. "Where you been?"

"Busy," Nick replied. "How's that shoulder?"

"Wrecked! I never knew touch football could be so rough." He looked at Sharyn. "Hey, who's this? I don't think I recognize the uniform."

"Bobby, Sharyn. Sharyn, Bobby."

"You a therapist or something?" Bobby wondered.

"She's the sheriff, you moron," Nick told him. "Don't you read the paper?"

Bobby looked at her closely. "I recognize you. You're running against that old geezer, right?"

"Right," she agreed, for the sake of argument.

He nodded and grinned. "That's what I thought. Hey! You're a lot better looking in person. Those cameras and stuff don't do you justice."

"Thanks."

"So, what'll it be?"

Nick caught Sharyn's eye. "Trust me?"

She shrugged. There didn't seem to be any menus. Maybe it was too straining for doctors to read from them. "Okay."

"Two of the usual," Nick ordered. "With that stuff you call wine instead of beer."

"Okay. Hey, good meeting you, Sheriff," Bobby told her.

"Thanks."

When they were alone, Nick looked at her. Should he bring it up? It wasn't really a big deal. What would he say? *Sharyn, about that kiss the other night when you were hurt...* He sipped his water.

"That was interesting," Sharyn began, filling in the silence between them. "The handwriting thing, I mean." Wasn't this the awkwardness that she had been trying to avoid by not getting involved with him? Of course, when *didn't* she feel awkward with him? "I agree with you though. I'd rather have a good, clear print to take to court."

Nick picked up a piece of bread and held it between his long fingers. "Why wouldn't Paul Reynolds give his prints and his blood if he didn't do it?" *Fall back on the case,* he thought defensively. It was easier than discussing something personal.

"I don't know," she admitted, taking a piece of bread and lightly touching it to the olive oil mixture. "He's been strange the whole time. I have to admit that he was the first person I thought of when the roof fell in on me. He warned me away from the place. Now with knowing about his past and his possible connection with the victim—"

"At least one of the victims," Nick reminded her.

Sharyn shrugged. "Well, a connection to either one of them is more than we had before. My grandfather was baffled by the whole thing. And I think he believed, at least a little bit, that the place was haunted and cursed. That's why he closed it down."

"How did Reynolds react when you told him the girl had been murdered?"

"I felt like he was hiding something. The way I've felt since I met him."

"You've got good instincts. Maybe you should trust them."

"I can't make him tell me the truth, though. And

without a confession or a print match, I've got zip. Even if he *did* know Betsy Peterson."

"That should be easy to tell with the prints I have. Whoever it was didn't care about leaving something behind."

"Still, there's a difference between threatening and doing. There's a big difference between pulling a gun on someone and actually shooting it," she explained. "It takes a whole different level of commitment."

Bobby brought their dinner and two glasses of the pale blush wine. They ate their pasta in silence for a few moments, while the restaurant grew more crowded around them.

"You've shot people," Nick said finally, sipping his wine.

"I have," she agreed. "That's how I know it's different."

"I don't know if everyone would agree with your psychology," Nick said.

"No. Some of the people we've arrested for murder wouldn't have thought about it any differently. But most people aren't killers. They can't cross that line so easily."

"How about you?" he asked, looking intently into her face as he spoke. "Was it hard for you to cross that line?"

"Yes," she admitted with a deep breath. "It was

hard. When I fired that shot that took down one of my father's killers, I thought I would hear the report forever." She looked back at him. "How about you?"

He looked away and started playing with what was left of his dinner. "Well, I—"

Sharyn sat back. "You haven't ever shot anyone, have you? With all those guns?"

Nick pressed his napkin to his lips. "No. I've never shot anyone. I practice at the range, but I haven't actually been involved with a case yet where I got to fire a gun."

She nodded. "It's not like it's necessary. I could've gone my whole life without shooting another living person. It's not the best part of the job."

"What is?"

"I don't know." She glanced around at the crowd and shrugged. "Feeling like I make a difference, I guess. I know that sounds corny."

"I don't think so. But I thought it was for the great parking places and Jack Winter's undivided attention."

Sharyn laughed lightly. "Yeah, right! I don't know what I did that made him so interested in me but I wish I could take it back."

Nick held her gaze. "I think he finds you attractive. And he wants to own you."

She looked away, grateful when Bobby came back for their plates. "What about you?" she asked him when the waiter had gone. "Why do you work as a medical examiner?"

"I've always liked dead people better than living ones," he remarked. "They don't talk back. They don't complain. They don't try to take your plate while you're still eating."

"Seriously," she prodded. "I know you could just teach forensics."

"It's the secrets, I suppose," he said after a moment. "I like finding the answers to puzzles. Each body they bring to me has its secrets. I like finding out what they are."

She believed him. For once, there wasn't any sarcasm in his tone. He had expressed himself straightforwardly, and now he smiled at her in a way that made her feel that he hadn't meant to reveal that much of himself.

He looked around the restaurant. "I guess we should be going. It's getting late."

"I can drive myself home, Nick," she said firmly. "I'll take my time. There's not much traffic. Can I drop you somewhere?"

Sharyn dropped him off at his office in the hospital. He went inside to get his things, but he was restless, and couldn't imagine going to sleep yet. Being with Sharyn had that effect on him. He had probably aged more than the normal amount in the past three and a half years just because he couldn't sleep after he'd been around her.

For two years after they had met, he'd lay in bed at night, thinking about her and how much she annoyed him. All those copper curls, and those blue eyes. He'd thought that he was just annoyed because she was the new sheriff. It took him two long years to realize how he *actually* felt about her. By that time, it was too late, and he was in bed at night thinking about her in other ways that tortured him.

He walked back to the sheriff's office in the cold, black, spring night. The fitful rain had given way to stars that danced above him, and a sliver of moon showed at the edge of Diamond Mountain. There was no staff at the office, only the automated switchboard, but he understood Sharyn's filing system. It was simple to find all of her notes on the case.

He sat in her chair, in her office, and read them thoroughly. They were clear and concise, but there were too many question marks. There was a map on her desk that caught his attention. He looked at it, turning it over and over before he realized that it was a map of the campground. It wasn't until he'd looked at it for the third time that his tired mind picked up on what was bothering him about it. He realized that Sharyn couldn't have seen it yet.

Nick looked up at the picture of T. Raymond

Howard. They had been friends as well as close working partners. He was a good man who worked hard at his job and loved his family.

He recalled the first time he'd met Sharyn. He had just moved to Diamond Springs from New York to get as far away from his past as possible. He had been amazed at the little town with its smiling people and clear, clean water and air.

Sharyn had been home from college on a break. She was arguing with her father about something, passionately defending whatever she believed in, as always. T. Raymond had been sitting back in his chair and smiling at her indulgently. When she'd finished, he nodded and acknowledged that he believed she might be right, but the burden of proof was on her shoulders.

T. Raymond had looked up and seen Nick at the door. He'd introduced the two of them. Sharyn just looked at him like he was Ernie or Joe or Ed. At the time, it hadn't bothered him. She was just a kid. After that, he'd met a few of her boyfriends and heard a few more of her arguments with her father. Their paths didn't cross much until that terrible day that T. Raymond had been shot. He'd done the autopsy on his friend. Later, he'd heard that his daughter was going to run for office in her father's place.

Nick picked up the heavy black phone and called the sheriff.

"The devil walks in Bell's Creek. I never had a doubt of it. He's laughing at me now, like he's laughed at others before me. It's not so bad to face retirement. Lots of days out on the lake. Time to whittle and see the seasons change. I'm just a man. I did the best I could against an inhuman foe. I will always hear that laughter."

SHARYN SAT UP in bed and rubbed her eyes. She wished she had read the romance instead of picking up her grandfather's journal before she went to sleep. She recalled Jacob as being a man of decision and action. The last entries in his journal showed him as being old and worn. It was hard reading his words at the close of his career.

Of course, he'd worked hard for thirty years as the sheriff when she was a kid, she'd heard the stories about him being shot and kicked and almost hanged once. He'd actually ridden a horse to patrol the county for most of his life.

She picked up the gun that had belonged to him from her bedside table. She could have chosen to carry her father's gun when she'd become sheriff. But she hadn't been able to make herself do that so close on the heels of his death. Her grandfather's weapon was old, but serviceable. It was heavier than the more modern weapons she could have carried. She had chosen to work with his gun because she'd been afraid. Just the thought of him handling the gun had given her courage to face the job as sheriff.

But he was superstitious, and he'd let his fears about the Devil's Campground area and Bell's Creek take over his investigation. The girl had been killed in a strange way, with the room locked and barred. She was sure that it was a terrible thing to find a young girl dead. Yet, the lack of evidence and even the paperwork was sloppy. Jacob's answer had been to close down the camp and hope for the best. She was paying the price for it twenty-five years later.

She knew Jacob wasn't a coward. He honestly believed there were things beyond his comprehension, things that couldn't be handled by a human because they were evil.

The phone rang and Sharyn threw back the sheet to answer it. "Yes?"

"Something bad has happened at the campground, Sheriff," David told her in an excited voice. "You better get down here quick!"

TEN

Sharyn didn't bother to put on her uniform. She added a coat and gloves, and slipped her feet into socks and boots. *I knew I shouldn't have let that place re-open.*

She got on the phone with Ed, Joe, and Ernie. She couldn't find Nick. She tried to call Kristie at the camp, but didn't get a reply. She realized that her sister was probably too busy with the children to answer the phone. J.P. answered when she tried his phone.

"What's happened?" she asked, bracing for the worst.

"One of the girls in the cabins was hurt," the deputy told her. "The paramedics just got here. They think it's knife wounds."

Sharyn felt a chill go down her spine. "How is she?"

"They think she'll be okay. One of the other girls in the cabin heard something and woke the counselor. She must have scared the guy off. He ran past her and slashed her arm, but they said she should be okay, too."

"What about the attacker?"

"No sign of him when we got here," J.P. told her. "David is tracking him now. He called in a man with a team of dogs."

"Okay. I'm only a few minutes away," she said. The taste of anger and defeat was bitter in her mouth. Was that the same taste her grandfather had reacted to when he refused to run for sheriff again after the last case at the campground? "Maybe that place really is evil."

"Sheriff?"

"Nothing. Just try to keep everyone from panicking. Let's not let him get away this time."

She reached the scene at the same time that Ernie arrived. "My phone's dead," he told her. "I picked it up from my pager. What's up?"

"Another attack," Sharyn told him. "I'm going to try to find J.P. and David. When Joe and Ed get here, keep them close at hand. We're going to want to get the children out of here as soon as we can."

"Sure."

The camp was full of lights and crying children. Sharyn found J.P. on the phone with David. The dogs were running through the woods, following a warm trail that would probably take them to the killer.

"Cabin three," J.P. directed Sharyn.

The little girl and the counselor were being taken

away in ambulances. The counselor's wound was only superficial. Sharyn kept her there for a few extra minutes. The little girl, Dinah Marquette, was too badly injured to take any chances. The paramedics left with her, the siren and lights echoing through the silence and fog that shrouded the camp.

"I don't know, Sheriff," the counselor told her. "It happened so fast. Allison came to get me because she thought a monster was trying to get Dinah. I looked over there. I shouted. He came past me. He cut me as he went by."

"What did he look like?"

"Tall. A lot taller than me." The woman started crying. "It hurt. He cut my arm. I screamed. Dinah and Allison were crying. Then the other girls started screaming. I just don't know where he went or what he looked like."

"Thanks anyway," Sharyn said, then looked at the paramedic. "She can go now. Let me know how the two of them are doing, please. Refer their doctors to my office. Thanks."

Sharyn looked around the camp. Parents were already showing up, and buses were being loaded. *Just like before,* she thought. She saw a bleary-eyed Caison Talbot getting out of his car. Reed Harker was already there. The press was getting as much footage as they could out of the incident.

There were too many people around the camp. It

might make it impossible to catch the killer. They were in danger of making the same mistakes that had been made twenty-five years ago. If that happened, the attacker would go free again.

"J.P.," she addressed her deputy, "we have to hold the line. These reporters and visitors can't be allowed into the camp. Get out the crime scene tape. I don't want the scene any more contaminated than it is already."

A bus driver started to plow right through the campsite.

"Hey, get that out of here," Sharyn told him, slapping the side of the bus. "Back it up!"

"I have to get the children!"

"I don't care! I'm the sheriff. This is a crime scene. Get it out of here!"

The parents and reporters were another thing. J.P. was putting up the tape, but they were ignoring it, pushing under it and trying to find their children. Ed and Joe showed up and added their voices and bodies to keep people out of the campground.

"Let's move the kids out of here rather than the parents in," she told them. "No reporters! In case he's still here, we don't want to lose him."

"Sheriff?" Foster Odom asked, coming up on her. "What's going on? What happened?"

"There's been another attack. You can't come into the campground. The slasher might still be here."

"What about the kids?"

"We're sending them out to meet their parents. We're emptying the camp, but we don't want to lose anything on the attacker before we can find him."

"Do you know who it is?" he asked.

"Not yet. There are dogs out tracking, but nothing yet."

"Sharyn!" Caison greeted her. "Why can't these parents go in and get their children?"

"Because the attacker might still be in there. We're sending their children out to them. I can't be responsible for anyone else being in the campground area. You shouldn't be here, Senator!"

"Nonsense! I'm supposed to be where my people are having trouble."

"Well, be on the other side of the tape for them. Please, sir. You're an example for everyone else. Do your part. Please."

The senator stepped back and reassured a few of his constituents before he addressed himself to the television cameras.

"This is a nightmare," Ed said, shaking his head. "I can't believe it could happen again the same way."

"Not the same way," Sharyn added. "We're here faster. The girl isn't dead. We're going to get the one responsible this time."

Everything Sharyn had been reading in her grandfather's diary about the crime and the aftermath raced through her mind. It *was* the same person. The dogs had tracked through the woods for days after the first murder. They had gone around in circles, never finding anything. Meanwhile, Betsy Peterson's killer had dumped Betsy's body and her suitcase. They had never thought to look for her and never found Rebecca's killer.

This time they were on the scene sooner. This time they had more sophisticated ways of finding a person and the truth.

Nick and Ernie found Sharyn. "There was a lot of blood, but I think it was all the little girl's blood," Nick told her. "We found the place where the attacker slashed the counselor. We got a nice shoe print from where he stepped in her blood. There's bound to be some prints."

"No sign of any weapon, though, Sheriff," Ernie reported. "We sealed off cabin number three so no one goes in. We'll get the devil this time."

"I brought this with me," Nick told her, taking out the map of the campground. "Look at those empty boxes drawn into the cabins."

"What are those?" she asked.

"What about secret rooms? Maybe that was another way to fool the devil."

Sharyn realized that she might have stumbled on one of the rooms that day at cabin five.

"Let's check it out," Ernie suggested. "Should be easy enough to tell."

"Sharyn! Sharyn!" her mother hailed her, crossing under the police tape. "Where's Kristie? I've been calling her and there's no answer. I've seen some counselors leave. Where's your sister?"

"We've gotten everyone out of the cabins and ready to go out by the parking lot," Joe told Faye. "The reporters are giving us the hardest time. The parents are just waiting for their kids."

"All the cabins are empty?" Sharyn asked, starting to walk past him towards the buses that were lined up and ready to leave. An icy chill was shaking her from within. She walked as fast as her injured leg would allow over the uneven ground. She thought she saw Kristie, but it was Kristie's friend, Amber.

"Have you seen Kristie?" she asked the girl.

"No," she said, crying. "I got out of there." She looked around. "Where is she? Where's Keith?"

"Keith?"

"Yeah. He was here for a while, but he said he couldn't stay. He came back to talk to her and they argued. I didn't see him leave. Is he still here? I don't see Kristie!"

"Sharyn!" her mother cried at her side. "Where is she?"

Sharyn swallowed hard, resisting the urge to

panic. She spoke to Ed calmly, having him go back through half of the cabins while she had Joe take the other half. She wanted to be there herself, but her knee made her slow and clumsy.

"We're looking for Keith Reynolds and Kristie," she told Joe. "The crowd's backed off some since the kids are out of the camp. Keith and Kristie are still missing."

Faye Howard started crying. The senator put his arm around her shoulders. "They'll find her. She's probably just rounding up the last of the kids or something."

Sharyn's phone rang. It was David. "The dogs are going around in circles out here. They lost the scent. I think the attacker might have run through the creek, at least along the edge of it, to get the scent off."

"Come back along the edge of the creek," she decided. "Keep an eye open in case he might still be out there. See if the dogs can pick up the smell again. I've sent for the helicopter. I just don't know if it will do much good before it gets light."

"Okay."

"I can't believe you didn't bring in that Reynolds boy for questioning," he remarked. "Nice move! It looks like he might have your sister now!" the senator roared.

"Don't be ridiculous, Senator," Sharyn scoffed.

"If Keith is out here, he might be in just as much danger as Kristie."

"But you don't know that, do you?" Faye Howard demanded. "He could have her. He could be the one who did this terrible thing again."

"Go back to the senator's car, Mom, and wait, please," Sharyn instructed her tersely. "When we know something, we'll tell you. In the meantime, you're just in the way."

"Don't speak to your mother that way," Caison growled.

Sharyn glared at him. "I can't do my job if I'm standing here talking to the two of you," she debated. "Take my mother to the car and I'll tell you when I know something else."

"Sharyn!" her mother cried.

"Please, Mom." She tried to get her mother to see reason. "Please trust me and wait until I know something else. We'll find Kristie."

The senator and her mother finally subsided and went back to the senator's long black car. A few reporters lined up around it, trying to get some answers from them.

"There's no one in those cabins," Joe reported breathlessly. "If this is a copycat, he's good."

"Especially since we haven't released anything about the Peterson girl's killing," Ed added. "Looks like he's following the same path."

"But where is he?" Sharyn questioned. She went back over everything her grandfather had learned when he was investigating. "How did he get away last time and this time?"

"We found two of the hidden rooms!" Nick yelled to them. "Ernie thinks he found a third!"

"Hidden rooms?" Joe asked. "These places were built so crazy, they could be anywhere."

"Nick has a map of the campground that show the rooms," Sharyn told him.

"They're not exact, but we were able to find some of them," Nick added.

"At least he won't be getting away while we're looking," Sharyn said. "J.P., I hate to have you work overtime but we don't have any choice. You and Joe cover this area. Watch for any movement. I think the chances are that he's still here. Ed, you and I will start helping Ernie and Nick look through the cabins. I don't care if we have to tear them apart. If he's hiding here, I want to know about it."

"How are we going to find these secret rooms?" Joe asked, following her closely as she walked towards the first cabin.

"Push at everything in the cabin. Make sure nothing moves, lifts, or falls in."

Cari's pretty blue Camaro pulled up as they were spreading out through the camp. "Sheriff!"

she called out, running from her car. "I've got Paul Reynolds with me!"

Sharyn walked back to meet her. "What is he doing here?"

"You need him," Cari told her, shaking with nerves and cold. "He knows something else he wasn't telling."

Sharyn looked at the man. "What is it, Mr. Reynolds?"

"My father," Paul Reynolds told her. "It's my father."

"What?"

He shook his head, wiping tears from his face with his sleeve. "He killed Elizabeth. He killed the little girl to hide it. He killed her because he thought she was going to ruin my life. He wanted me to take over his church so much that he wasn't willing to take a chance. I didn't know. I swear I didn't know. I don't know how he found out that she was pregnant. He thought she was pregnant when he killed her. He thought he'd taken care of the whole thing."

He swayed on his feet and paused for breath. "I didn't know about Keith when the foundling home that had taken care of him closed down. There's a rare genetic condition that's passed from father to son in my family. When I learned that Keith had it ten years ago, I had us both tested. I didn't tell him the truth."

"What about your father?" Sharyn asked him.

"He's not well. He forgets. He thinks Keith is me. I think he sees it happening all over again because the camp reopened after all these years. He's going through the same thing but this time, he thinks your sister is Elizabeth. He called her that before."

Sharyn swallowed hard. "He wants to kill Kristie?"

"I don't know. I don't think he'll hurt anyone else. But I know this place. I can find anything here. Let me look for him. I should have told you the truth. I thought I could protect him. I just wanted to scare you when I pushed the cabin in, Sheriff. I hoped everyone would go away. Now, I just want to make things right."

"Where's Keith, Mr. Reynolds?"

"I don't know. He should have been with Dad."

"Kristie brought him here tonight. Now he's gone."

"He's not involved in any of this!"

"Are you sure?"

"I'm sure! Please, Sheriff! Let me find my father! He might even have Keith with him!"

Sharyn considered his words. She couldn't afford to waste any time. "All right. You can come with me. Cari, you take up a position to watch the camp perimeter."

"Okay."

"You did the right thing, Cari."

Cari smiled, relieved. "Thanks, Sheriff."

Sharyn and Joe walked towards the cabins, nestled in the trees.

"Where were the girls hurt, Sheriff?" the pastor asked her.

"Cabin number three," she answered. "Are there any secret rooms in there?"

"No. But there is a secret room in cabin four. Since they're side by side, it's possible he could be in there."

Sharyn took out her grandfather's service revolver.

"Please, Sheriff. Please try not to hurt him. He's old and sick."

"I won't make any promises," Sharyn replied. "He's killed twice and tried to kill again last night." *And he has my sister,* she wanted to scream at the man.

"He's probably confused," Paul told her. "If we can reach him before he does anything else, it should be all right."

It should be all right. All the possibilities rang through her mind as they walked to the next cabin. She pushed aside the idea that Kristie could already be dead, like Betsy. That wasn't going to happen.

The camp was empty except for people with the sheriff's department. Paul walked to the side of the cabin and pushed hard at a window. It opened slowly to reveal a small dark room. "Dad, are you in here? Dad?"

There was no answer, but the dust that lay undisturbed on the wooden floor was its own reply.

"What about another cabin?"

He nodded. "Cabin seven. It has an extra room."

"What was the idea of the extra rooms?" Sharyn asked as they hurried to the next cabin.

"They were rooms where children were punished. It was an easy way to deal with the bad children without hurting the good ones."

She was appalled. "They were closed in these rooms?"

"Yes. My grandfather remembered it well. It seems he always had trouble being good. There was a way to lock the room from the outside." He demonstrated with the secret room in cabin seven. "They couldn't get out once they were locked in."

When they opened the door, someone rushed at them. It was Keith. His glasses were gone and he was filthy. "He's got Kristie!" he told them wildly. "He thought I was you, Dad! He told me that he was going to take care of some problem. I thought I could talk to him, then he locked me in here."

"Keith!"

"No!" He pushed away from his father. "We have

to find them! He's crazed, Dad, you don't understand! I'm afraid he's going to hurt Kristie!"

"No! Not again!" his father cried in anguish.

"What do you mean?" Keith asked him, bewil-
dered. When his father couldn't reply, he turned to
Sharyn. "We have to find them."

"We'll find her." Sharyn assured him as much
as herself. "Where's the next cabin with a secret
room, Pastor?"

"Number twelve, closest to the creek," Paul said.

"Hurry!" Keith urged.

Sharyn called it in to the other deputies on her
cell phone. David was back with the dogs and the
search team. They were all converging on their lo-
cation.

The sky was just getting light beyond the heavy
forest, across the Uwharrie Mountains. Diamond
Mountain stood like a squat giant in the background, swathed in mist, while the rest of the gen-
tle peaks rolled off to the sides.

They started to walk to the cabin, but Sharyn's
eye caught movement in the forest towards the creek
side. "There!" she told them, moving quickly even
though her knee responded painfully.

"Dad!"

"Stop him!" Keith yelled. "He's got Kristie!"

The figure stopped, and then began to move

again. He was dragging something heavy and cumbersome behind him.

"Stop now, Mr. Reynolds," Sharyn said in a cold, clear tone that echoed off the trees. Her hand gripped her gun. She had a solid shot that was well above Kristie's head and torso but it would mean hitting Ezekiel Reynolds in the head or chest. Joe stood behind her with his own gun drawn.

Ezekiel stopped once more. She couldn't clearly see his face in the dim light. He was silhouetted against the steadily lightening sky.

"Dad!" Paul called out to his father. "Please, don't let this happen!"

"Go away! It's too late! You've sinned and God will judge you! But you are my son and you will be the pastor of our church! This little harlot won't stop you now!"

"You're wrong, Dad! Please! Please come back now!"

Ezekiel started moving again. Sharyn took a deep breath and squeezed the trigger. The report in the quiet forest was nearly as loud as the one she'd described to Nick. The sound echoed for long moments while nothing moved. Finally, he fell.

Paul and Keith Reynolds scrambled through the forest to reach him, but Ezekiel toppled into the foaming rapids of Bell's Creek. His head disappeared beneath the water, and he was washed away in the current before they could reach him. Paul dropped to his knees and buried his head in his hands. Keith ran back to where he'd dropped Kristie.

Sharyn knelt at Kristie's side. She had a deep puncture wound in her neck and chest. Her clothes were soaked with blood. Sharyn's hands were shaking as she got on her cell phone and demanded a paramedic unit. Nick was at her side before she could put down the phone. Ed, Joe, and Ernie were walking the banks of the creek looking for any sign of Ezekiel. They met David and J.P. with the dogs, trying to decide if the man had survived.

"She'll be okay," Nick told Sharyn after he'd looked at Kristie. "She's lost some blood but she'll be okay."

"Good."

He glanced at her. "Are you all right?"

"Yes."

"Did you kill him?"

"Probably. There was no other way to take the shot without endangering Kristie."

"You did what you had to do," Ernie said, coming back to them. "The old man's probably down to the dam already, the way this current is running. It'll be a miracle if we find his body."

"Like Betsy," Sharyn said, realizing that she was still holding her grandfather's gun. She put it away.

Kristie moaned and opened her eyes. "Sharyn?"

"I'm here," her sister said, taking her hand. "Nick says you're going to be okay. The paramedics are coming. You'll be out of here in no time, Kristie. Just hang on."

Kristie smiled feebly. "That man, Keith's grand-father—" She shuddered. "He kept calling me Elizabeth. He told me I was ruining his life."

"That's enough talking now," Nick said firmly. "You can talk later. Just rest for now, Kristie. Conserve your strength."

"Thanks, Nick. I love you, Sharyn. How's it feel to always be right?"

IT WAS A MONTH LATER when Faye Howard invited the entire sheriff's office to Sunday dinner at her home. She wanted to thank them for saving her daughter. The weather had warmed by then, and the grass was green. The azaleas were blooming, pink and white, all over the yard.

Every deputy was wearing his or her pager, ready to leave if something came up. But it was Sunday, and Diamond Springs liked to sleep in on Sunday and eat dinner after church. There was a volunteer patrol on duty in case anything happened. Gathered around the big table in Faye Howard's backyard, everyone was feeling good.

"To the sheriff's office of Diamond Springs,

Montgomery County, North Carolina!" David said, raising his glass of lemonade. He smiled at Cari, who sat beside him. She looked away, catching Ed's eye and smiling shyly.

"How's Kristie doing?" Ernie asked Sharyn, looking at the other girl who sat beside her mother at the far end of the table.

Sharyn sighed. "She's too quiet. It's not like her. I've tried to get her to go to counseling but she refuses. She won't go back to school. She and Keith broke up last week. She said it wasn't anything personal, but she just couldn't see him without thinking about that day at the campground."

Nick nodded. "No wonder Keith has been useless around the morgue. He didn't say anything. I thought maybe he changed his mind about assisting me."

"I'm worried about Kristie," Sharyn admitted. "The doctor says she's healed but I think her mind hasn't caught up with her wounds yet."

"Caison has had a tough time taking the blame for the whole thing, hasn't he?" Ernie asked with a half-smile, noticing that the senator was absent from the party. "Nice to see him getting some heat for a change."

"He pushed hard for the camp to re-open," Joe remarked. "He wanted the glory if it worked.

The press is crucifying him for not agreeing with the sheriff."

"Never did find the old pastor's body," Ed interjected, swallowing a mouthful of coleslaw. "That place is still pretty spooky, if you ask me."

"Yeah, well, it won't be there to re-open again," Joe stated flatly. "I went out there after the fire last week. There's nothing out there but some charred timber."

Ed nodded his curly blond head. "That was pretty mysterious, too."

Ernie rubbed his chin. "Not as mysterious as all that. The Gazette reported that 'several concerned citizens' finally took the law into their own hands to prevent another tragedy. I think somebody knows who did it, and it wasn't the devil!"

"Considering that was county property," Sharyn added. "I hope it always stays a mystery."

"Don't think you have to worry about that, Sheriff," Ernie remarked. "If somebody torched the old campground, it's not likely they're gonna come forward."

"It was nice of Commissioner Sommers to point out to everyone that you tried to keep the camp closed," Nick said to Sharyn. "And nice of the D.A. to agree to reduce the charges against Keith's father to attempted manslaughter. I'm sure he has some motive besides his inherent generosity."

"It was the right thing," Sharyn stated. "Kristie

is okay, and the little girl is fine. He'll still do time. Not that he'll live another day without suffering from what happened. He just wanted to protect his father, despite the horrible thing the old man did."

"You know, Keith moved out and won't speak to him," Nick said quietly. "He's sleeping at the hospital. He's not going back to school for a while either."

"I'd say the devil had his due on this one," Ed offered.

"I have a toast I'd like to make," Selma Howard said, coming from the house with another bowl of potato salad. She picked up her glass of lemonade and smiled at her niece. "To my niece, Sharyn Howard. She preserved our family homestead and beat the devil at his own game!"

Everyone drank to the toast, but no one knew what she was talking about.

"The state was going to tear down my house for the new highway. As you all know, the judge was lenient with me for having hurt that poor state worker—which I had no business doing, but I was just beside myself with grief. I asked my niece for help because she's the sheriff and I didn't care if she had to bend the rules to save our house." She winked at Sharyn. "But you know she was so smart and so slick, she thought of another way to save the property without doing more than hiring a lawyer to look into it."

"What happened?" Trudy asked.

"The Howard property is now officially an historic landmark. It was there right in front of my nose the whole time. I just couldn't see it. With that designation—which I assure you the house and land deserve—the state will protect the house instead of plowing through it. We'll lose some land but the house stays. And that's the end of that."

Sharyn smiled and sipped her lemonade. "I was inspired when you told me that it would be mine someday."

Everyone laughed.

"Well your father and your grandfather and all the other Howard generations before you are proud of you." Selma waggled her eyebrows.

"That was pretty clever," Nick conceded, looking at Sharyn.

"Thanks," Sharyn replied with a soft smile.

"Slick. That's what I'm gonna start calling her," Ernie remarked. "Sheriff Slick."

"It's because she was almost a lawyer," Ed said. "But she was too good for them."

"Speech!" Joe yelled, clapping.

"Speech!" The chant was picked up around the table.

Sharyn held up her hand. Her cheeks were blushing a deep red and she refused to get to her feet.

"Well, if she won't speak," her mother said. "I have a few things I'd like to say."

The people around the table grew quiet.

"I know all of you know me. I know most of you know I didn't ever like T. Raymond being the sheriff here, and I certainly didn't ever want my daughter to be the sheriff! How could anything be further from a mother's mind?"

Sharyn had her hands in her lap. She looked at her plate, praying that her mother wasn't going to be too embarrassing in what she had to say about the whole thing. She felt Ernie touch her left hand, taking it firmly in his own. She looked up. He winked at her and nodded.

Nick's warm hand crept to hers on the right, holding it gently. She looked at him and he looked back at her, his eyes daring her to say anything about the support he was silently offering her.

She squeezed both of their hands and looked up at her mother where she stood at the head of the table. Selma Howard was advancing towards Faye, with a ladle in one hand, in case the talk turned ugly.

"But my daughter is the sheriff of this county," Faye continued. "I won't ever be any happier about it. She manages to put her life on the line all the time." She drew a deep breath and looked at Sharyn.

"But you've saved so many lives already, and the people in this town deserve the best. That's what you are, Sharyn. You are the best sheriff this town could have. You saved your sister's life." Her pretty blue eyes clouded and her lips trembled. "I plan to cast my vote in November for Sheriff Sharyn Howard. She's what this county needs." She lifted her glass. "How about the rest of you?"

Everyone around the pleasantly shaded table applauded. Sharyn's eyes filled with tears. She knew it took a lot for her mother to swallow her pride that way. She didn't know what to say, although everyone was looking at her to speak.

Finally, when everyone grew quiet, she got to her feet. "This case broke my grandfather's spirit twenty-five years ago. He believed he couldn't help the county anymore if he couldn't find this killer. My father was a deputy at the time, but he wouldn't run for office because he was worried that he didn't have enough experience. So he let Roy Tarnower win the election. When Roy did such a poor job that T. Raymond thought anyone would be better, he ran against him and beat him in the next election. I guess I can't let that tradition die now."

Everyone applauded, and Ernie hugged her. Ed wrapped his arms around both of them. Nick sat back, wishing it could be that easy and spontaneous for him.

"To the next sheriff of Montgomery County," Joe said, standing. "Watch out, Roy Tarnower!"

* * * * *

REQUEST YOUR FREE BOOKS!

2 FREE NOVELS
PLUS 2 FREE GIFTS!

WORLDWIDE LIBRARY®
Your Partner in Crime

ReaderService.com

Manage your account online!

- Review your order history
- Manage your payments
- Update your address

*We've designed
the Harlequin® Reader Service
website just for you.*

Enjoy all the features!

- Reader excerpts from any series
- Respond to mailings and
  special monthly offers
- Discover new series available to you
- Browse the Bonus Bucks catalog
- Share your feedback

Visit us at:
ReaderService.com

REQUEST YOUR
FREE BOOKS!

2 FREE NOVELS
FROM THE SUSPENSE COLLECTION
PLUS 2 FREE GIFTS!

YES! Please send me 2 FREE novels from the Suspense Collection and my 2 FREE gifts (gifts are worth about $10). After receiving them, if I don't wish to receive any more books, I can return the shipping statement marked "cancel." If I don't cancel, I will receive 4 brand-new novels every month and be billed just $5.99 per book in the U.S. or $6.49 per book in Canada. That's a savings of at least 25% off the cover price. It's quite a bargain! Shipping and handling is just 50¢ per book in the U.S. and 75¢ per book in Canada.* I understand that accepting the 2 free books and gifts places me under no obligation to buy anything. I can always return a shipment and cancel at any time. Even if I never buy another book, the two free books and gifts are mine to keep forever.

191/391 MDN FVVK

Name	(PLEASE PRINT)	
Address		Apt. #
City	State/Prov.	Zip/Postal Code

Signature (if under 18, a parent or guardian must sign)

Mail to the Harlequin® Reader Service:
IN U.S.A.: P.O. Box 1867, Buffalo, NY 14240-1867
IN CANADA: P.O. Box 609, Fort Erie, Ontario L2A 5X3

Want to try two free books from another line?
Call 1-800-873-8635 or visit www.ReaderService.com.

* Terms and prices subject to change without notice. Prices do not include applicable taxes. Sales tax applicable in N.Y. Canadian residents will be charged applicable taxes. Offer not valid in Quebec. This offer is limited to one order per household. Not valid for current subscribers to the Suspense Collection or the Romance/Suspense Collection. All orders subject to credit approval. Credit or debit balances in a customer's account(s) may be offset by any other outstanding balance owed by or to the customer. Please allow 4 to 6 weeks for delivery. Offer available while quantities last.

Your Privacy—The Harlequin® Reader Service is committed to protecting your privacy. Our Privacy Policy is available online at www.ReaderService.com or upon request from the Harlequin Reader Service.

We make a portion of our mailing list available to reputable third parties that offer products we believe may interest you. If you prefer that we not exchange your name with third parties, or if you wish to clarify or modify your communication preferences, please visit us at www.ReaderService.com/consumerschoice or write to us at Harlequin Reader Service Preference Service, P.O. Box 9062, Buffalo, NY 14269. Include your complete name and address.

SUS13

REQUEST YOUR FREE BOOKS!
2 FREE NOVELS PLUS 2 FREE GIFTS!

HARLEQUIN®

INTRIGUE®

BREATHTAKING ROMANTIC SUSPENSE

HIDIR13